# HOW TO NOT BE ALONE ON CHRISTMAS

A SWEET, CHRISTMAS DISASTER

CAMILLA EVERGREEN

*Reader Expectations*

**Heat Level**: Fade-to-black, innuendos, no cursing, sensual description, mentions of sex
**Notable Tropes**: Guy falls first, grumpy/sunshine, childhood friends to lovers, second chance, only one room at the inn, forced proximity
**Triggers**: apocalypse, duck named Jimmy, potatoes
**Style**: First person present, single POV
**Stress Level**: Low (unless you wrote it)
**Ending**: HEA

Edited by a Strange Little Squirrel
Cover Art by House of Orian Graphics

*For Instagram*
*Specifically, the ones who replied.*

❖

# ACKNOWLEDGMENTS

♥ You asked for this.

---

This story began when a silly child (me) asked sillier children (you) what Christmas was. I'd believe I was lied to if it all didn't make perfect sense. This book is for you guys, and Jimmy. Because obviously it's for Jimmy.

Thank you for your help in teaching me the true meaning of Christmas. I have done my best to make this book the Christmasiest Christmas book it can be by including every last suggestion I have been provided, no matter how difficult it has been to squish them all together. I hope you'll forgive me the tweaks I've made in order to keep this story logically within the series.

I'm half-certain the intention was to have me forfeit logic altogether.

But that simply will not do.

For I am a proper author, who does proper author things, and writes proper author books.

The following tale is brought to you thanks to the collective minds of mybooksandimaginations, brittnys.booktalk, ashafarless, sukainawriting, secretrhs05, fatimahs_queendom, regallywritten, shelvedthoughts, fierymermaidbooks, bookswith_brandi, queenemilyoreo, marionderewrites, a.messterpiece, and abbys.always.reading.

Merry Christmapocalypse to all, and to all Happy Reading.


P.S. For those of you who were not directly involved in the creation of this disaster, allow me to explain…

Once upon a time, I asked Instagram if I was supposed to write a Christmas story with the intention of siding with those who said "no." #TeamGrinch.

Nobody. Said. No.

My joke was positively foiled, so I started a different one and claimed I had no idea what a Christmas was. I asked for assistance on what belonged in a Christmas book.

The first person to respond said *Potatoes and Ducks*.

Clearly, I knew less about Christmas than I thought.

Things got out of hand from that point on, and I have made it my duty to accept every last bit of chaos without discretion. If you are coming into this story blind, it should still make sense. Enough of it, anyway. At least no less than romantic comedies normally do.

I have decided that the chapter titles for this book shall allude to the requests I was given more than they shall allude to the "tips" from Melanie Richards' books (as is a staple of this series, which you might want to read, because they are just as whimsical with about half the screaming).

I cannot, and will not, be held accountable for anything. Enjoy.

With Love, Lore, & Chaos,
Camilla Evergreen

# CHAPTER 1

♥ It is absolutely an "apocalypse," and there's totally a Christmas tree.

---

Christmapocalypse: Welcome to the Home of Christmas ~~Cheer~~ Fear.

Meet new people.

Enjoy classic festivities.

Survive.

The second I saw the flier in my door, I was contacting the retreat, sorting the details, and packing for my three-week stay at Gingerbread Inn, located snugly within the magical (albeit post-apocalyptic) village of Wintergreen, Florida.

I have never been this excited before in my life. Not that the bar is entirely high. Up until this point, my life has consisted of working from home as a website manager, reading, and waiting on a miracle. As an orphan who aged out of the system, I've spent a lot of time waiting on miracles, only to have the ones I thought I found fall through the cracks.

This is going to be different.

Because this *isn't* a miracle. It's a story I get to live in for three whole weeks. And if I've learned anything from my twenty-four years of life and books, stories may not always have happily ever afters, but they do tend to have more than a single-person cast, which is better than I've had since I graduated from high school five years ago and lost...*him*.

I don't like to think about *him*. Not anymore.

Some things are too hard to remember, and they'll ruin my cheer.

Standing in the ransacked lobby of Gingerbread Inn with a crowd of other eager participants, I am armed with a suitcase full of survival necessities (clothes, mostly), hope, and a book I have been studying in preparation for the biggest holiday of the year.

Melanie Richards' *How to Not Be Alone on Christmas* sits pretty in my duffle bag. The wealth of its knowledge together with this two-week adventure concluding on Christmas night is going to help me forget everything about Lover and Friends Past and get me looking toward Lover and Friends *Future* as I work on making them Lover and Friends Present, obviously.

It's the *perfect* plan! I let this whole "Christmapocalypse" event take care of the *plot elements*, and naturally I'll find my shy, awkward, and occasionally overly-bubbly self surrounded by people. A few of Melanie's tactics here and there, and I'll have a happily ever after by Christmas Day, where I will—for the first time in five years—*not* be alone, drinking eggnog (which is actually just straight rum), and crying into the tiny Christmas tree I buy because my five-foot-three, two-fifty pound self cannot safely get a real tree up the steps to my apartment.

Beaming helplessly, I glance at the massive Christmas tree in the corner of the turned-over lobby. It's glowing and blinking and covered star-to-trunk in shimmering ornaments. A lovely brick fireplace crackles across from it, homey, as though the couches and chairs that may have once been arranged neatly in front of it aren't flipped over and askew.

Above our heads, simple chandeliers flicker with eerie,

end-of-the-world promise, but the Christmas tree does not care as it brightens the space with pure, safe innocence. It's the most chaotic mashup of doom and joy I've ever seen, and I am living for it.

All the lights—Christmas tree included—turn off abruptly, and a short gasp spills out of me. The murmurs of my co-vacationers fizzle to a halt.

"Good evening, one and all!" A woman's voice fills the room, and I bite my tongue to keep from squealing when a spotlight hits the top of a set of carpeted steps leading up behind the dismantled inn reception desk. Pale hands spread wide, the woman's fir-green drop sleeves graze the floor. A knife belt strapped across her chest ends securely at the gun on her hip. Her red vinyl slacks dip into calf-high black heels, and all she's missing is a Santa hat atop her short auburn curls. "My name is Holly, and I will be your guide throughout this adventure. By this point, each of you should have already read, agreed to, and signed the waiver absolving our town of any…*unforeseen circumstances*. We care deeply about the health and safety of everyone present; however, due to the nature of our little game, the occasional spot of *trouble* does get in the way. I would like to take this moment to remind everyone that we are indeed playing a *game*, and if you cease to play nicely, your position in it shall be compromised without refund. If you seek to forfeit your spot peacefully at any time, you shall be reimbursed for a portion of the days you give up.

"Make no mistake…" Holly's green eyes flash, something about them unnaturally bright. "…these next few weeks will be about survival, and some of you may not make it out alive."

With those chilling words, a man near me coughs, gasps, and crumples. I startle away from where he hits the floor, grasping his chest. Eyes wide and irises red, like the

3

swirl of a candy cane, he draws his hand away from himself, and it shakes. Chocolate syrup drips from his fingers onto the floor in an ooze of star-shaped sprinkles.

Holly's grin widens, white and sparkling. "Don't worry about him. He'll be back with us shortly…in a different sort of way. The premise here in Wintergreen is very simple —due to the balance between Nice and Naughty shifting in drastic favor of Naughty, Santa Claus has taken it into his own hands to purge the world by turning the wicked into sentient candy beings capable only of joy. We are among the few who remain, and I'm certain we'll all be *perfectly fine*."

Two people dressed in green and red with bells on their spiky hats jingle out of a back room up to the man who has now gone still in a pile of chocolate syrup and peppermints. They pluck him up, and a trail of sprinkles drips ominously across the floor as they take him away.

Holy night.

No one told me this was a *fantasy* apocalypse dystopian story!

I'm vibrating now, biting my lip in a futile effort to mute my grin.

Holly glides down the steps, her boots crunching sprinkles and mints as she steps before us. "Santa's little helpers are everywhere, so do behave now that you've seen coal in your stocking is the least of your worries. Let's all have fun, shall we?" Her eyes catch on mine for a single moment, twinkling, and then the entire façade drops. The magical, chipper tone of her voice levels as she scans everyone else in the group. "It's my duty to remind you seriously that this town is occupied by staff and rescue animals. Do *not* feed the rescue animals anything that has not been cleared by a member of the staff. Any aggression or harm coming to either animals or staff will result in immediate charges as well as dismissal." Holly's entire expression deadpans. "Seriously, guys. It's Christmas. This world we've made *might* explode, and *some* people *might* be reborn as sentient candy, but if you give any of the kittens chocolate, I will end you personally."

There. Are. KITTENS?

Holly claps her hands and brightens as I internally squee. I *must* meet the kittens! These next few weeks are going to be the best days of my life.

Smiling sweetly once more, Holly extends a hand and displays the staircase she descended from. "Now, with all of that out of the way, welcome to the aftermath of the collapse of society. Christmas is imminent. Survival is optional. This evening, your most important task is locating where you'll be staying. Building alliances is encouraged. You might just need them." With that, a white and red explosion of smoke accompanies the death of the spotlight. Once the Christmas lights and flickering chandeliers turn back on, Holly is gone.

Oh. My. Christmas!!

Okay. I need to calm down.

"This is a trip and a half already." A young woman beside me laughs and brushes her dark hair behind her ear as she scoops up her suitcase. Heading toward the stairs with several other guests, she begins talking to a man beside her.

As the crowd around me thins, most heading toward the stairs, I realize…everyone is in pairs.

She's with him. He's with her. They're together. Those people are together. That couple is a *couple*. He's helping her with her suitcase. That person is suggesting they just claim the best bedroom they can find—it is a survival story, after all, first-come, first-serve.

A tiny prickle of dread takes root in my stomach.

It is almost *instantly* interrupted by a high-pitched voice chirping, "Hello!"

I lurch, spinning to find an elf. The petite woman's rocking on soft shoes that curl into fiddlehead tips. Touching my chest to settle my hammering heart, I smile and hope, you know, that this is not entirely a morbid "all the elves want to turn you into candy" story. Just a…"sometimes when you're bad they do" story. "Hello."

Her head tilts, a tiny bell piercing the tip of one pointed ear chiming. "You're Marigold, aren't you? You're our only guest who didn't bring a partner."

Ow. "Oh? Am I? I didn't see that this was a *couple's* thing on the flier I got."

The elf's pink lips pout, her much-too-bright red eyes taking on a sincere quality. "It isn't; however, a lot of our games do tend to be enjoyed more thoroughly in pairs, and you do not have a pair while everyone else does."

I've noticed life is also more thoroughly enjoyed in pairs, and…yeah…I don't have one.

Linking her arms behind her back, the elf grins. "It would be *such* a shame if you didn't enjoy yourself. It's positively *naughty* to not enjoy yourself during the most wonderful time of the year."

Oh no. I'm already being scouted to be turned into candy. Ha ha. And my loneliness is being used as the catalyst. Dude. Guys. Come on. It's *Christmas*. This is a Christmas thing. I'm literally going to cry here.

Swallowing the lump in my throat, I force my smile. "Don't worry. I'm used to keeping my spirits up by myself." I've been doing it for years, practically my entire life. AND I can still make friends even if everyone's already paired off as lovers. Making friends is a good start. Who says every story has to be a romance?

My Kindle library, that's who.

The elf's creepy smile falls. "Are you all right?"

Still smiling, I cock my head. "Hm? Of course." A droplet skates down my cheek, and I startle, lifting my hand to catch the tear, wipe it away. I sniff. "Sorry. I cry over everything. Happy and sad tears. I gave up on trying to wear makeup because literally anything can set me off and ruin it. Your makeup looks amazing, by the way."

The elf stares at me, her rosy cheeks and glittery eyelids perfectly magical and severely bright to accentuate her role. A small smile softens her pink lips, and she extends her hand. "Tessa Christmessa. Usually our guests are wary of us, so it's nice to have a friend."

I take her hand and grin through my tears. *A friend.* That is a good start. Yay. Right. Who said I needed to make friends with the other *humans*? I don't read fantasy romance for nothing, and the actors and actresses are people, too. All hope is not yet lost. Maybe my love story will be with one of the elves. "It's nice to meet you, Tessa. We weren't exactly told that Santa or his elves were *evil*, just that they were purging it, right? There's no need to be afraid or wary if I'm not doing anything wrong."

Her laughter is remarkably bell-like considering she isn't actually an elf. "We're turning people into candy monsters, Mari. We are *obviously* the antagonists in this story, but it is *never* too early to throw your lot in with the villains."

That's a good point followed by an even better one.

Flashing my teeth, I grin, and we beam at each other for an exciting moment, then it's my turn to laugh as I release her hand. "This is my first time doing anything like this. You have no idea how awesome it is to feel like I'm in an open world game. Is Santa Claus an actual character we'll get to see?"

Tessa drapes a finger against her lips. "Tut tut, Mari.

It's only the first night. I'm not supposed to ruin the story for you. But I can give you this." With flare, a green scarf explodes out of her hands, and she waves it away to reveal a little key in her palm.

I look down as she claps the simple silver item into my hand. "Sooner or later everyone else will realize they have to *find* their room keys before they can enter any of the rooms upstairs, but you're already my favorite, so I'm giving you the best suite." Conspiring, she holds a hand to one side of her mouth and whispers, "Also, the elevator totally works and everything is completely safe—despite appearances. You don't have to take the stairs all the way to Room 25, because there aren't any."

I smile, clasping the key to my chest. "Thank you so much, Tessa."

Dancing away from me, she giggles. "Thank *you* for spending time with us! And always remember: you might think a Christmapocalypse is off-brand for such a cheerful holiday, but it's actually way more true to the horrifying roots! You've been brainwashed by Hallmark! Santa is terrifying! In some cultures—"

Out of nowhere, a tall man with frosty white hair and long elven ears whacks Tessa in the back of the head, sighs, and lifts his fingers in greeting. "Ignore my little sister. She can get carried away."

I laugh, wiping the last of my tears. "It's all right. I love it."

The beautiful man smiles, bright blue eyes gentle. Aqua tints his sharp cheeks and full lips, everything about him screaming magic and other world—even though I know it's all makeup. Gracefully, he bows low. "Jack Frost, of course."

"You're an elf?" I ask as Tessa begins humming "Santa Claus Is Coming to Town," specifically at the *he sees you when you're sleeping* line.

"What are elves if not all winter's minions?" Jack Frost queries.

Footsteps start down the stairs behind me, a murmur of the other guests realizing they have to *find* their keys.

Jack sucks his teeth and directs a slender finger toward an elevator plucked out of a horror movie. The illuminated floor light winks on and off. "We're not supposed to interact with everyone yet. You better head on up to your room so we can disappear before the boss hears what we've done." Taking my free hand in his frigid one, Jack kisses my knuckles. "Charmed, Marigold. And welcome to Gingerbread Inn." He winks. "Let us know if you see anything naughty, all right?"

I don't know how they do it, but in the very next instant, the lights turn off, his cold touch pulls away, and the elves are gone, leaving nothing but a vaguely disturbing whisper of Christmas magic behind.

# CHAPTER 2

♥ There is a blizzard in Florida, and, lo, a childhood best friend is driving in it.

---

I. Love. My. *Room*.

I stand gaping just past the threshold for long minutes, staring in awe at the scene before me. Christmas threw up in here. It's *gorgeous*. I can hardly breathe, but when I manage the slightest inhale, it smells like evergreens, cinnamon, chocolate, and ginger.

The vast *pent house* of a room sprawls before me in shades of icy blue and white. Soft Christmas hymns play sweetly from surround-sound speakers. Dead ahead, a lit fireplace pours heat into the space, crackling a symphony that melds with the gentle music. A chandelier made of crystal hangs central above snowflake tile, and I wander—shivering—into the elegant suite.

On my left, two steps lead to a platform with a California King size bed draped in a dark lace canopy shimmering with glittering flecks. Frosted, tall windows displaying the quaint village of Wintergreen, Florida frame the nightstands.

On my right, a Christmas tree swallows an alcove adorned with an eclectic array of small tables. Every last table overflows with treats—cookies, brownies, cakes, chocolate, bottles of wine, cheeses on cooled and covered trays. Glass domes keep everything I can see fresh and secure.

I wander into the wonderland, covering my mouth as I

10

take every detail in.

Tinsel and tiny paper snowflakes. A platter of candies. Tiny gifts.

Biting my lip, I lift one little present and a laugh escapes. It's beautiful. All of it is beautiful. This entire room is more luxurious than I could hope to imagine, and I can't believe I'm staying here for only three thousand dollars. Twenty-four entire days in *this*, not counting tonight? I'd have paid more for a *normal* hotel room. I guess some good can come of being lonely.

First, because I was by myself, I ended up left in the lobby and meeting two elves—who basically invited me to join their dark side.

Um, thank you, yes.

Second, because I was all alone, Tessa Christmessa— best name ever, kudos to whoever put this thing together— gave me the coolest room. Room 25 is the *only* room on the top floor. I didn't see any stairs leading up here once I got out of the elevator, so I think it can only be reached by the truly terrifying and somewhat off-putting elevator.

It feels like I've been invited into the backstage of this adventure, and *how freaking epic is that?*

It's so settled. I'm making elf friends for the next twenty-four days. I'm not just going to *survive* this apocalypse, I'm going to thrive in it.

Turning the tiny gift over in my hand, I pinch a little card attached to the bow and read: *Open Me.*

Open it?

Really? It's so light, exactly like a fake wrapped gift for decoration.

My heart pounds as I turn the card over and find the other side has a tiny rabbit etched in silver embossed upon it.

Major *Alice in Wonderland* vibes, also known as my

11

favorite book. However, I'll feel somewhat guilty if I open it and I'm not actually supposed to. The display of food in this room alone probably costs as much as I've paid to be here. I don't want to destroy anything.

Setting the little gift back down beside a *glorious* array of petit fours, I conclude that I will ask one of my new elf friends about it later. For now, I am going to get my luggage unpacked and reference my *How to Not Be Alone on Christmas* book in order to make sure I don't mess up in the whole *making friends* or *flirting* departments.

Just in case I, you know, find any cute elves precariously placed beneath any mistletoe.

Jack Frost, for instance.

I wonder what he looks like without the white hair and makeup. He was so wonderfully tall.

Just like…

Giving my head a firm shake, I snatch a caramel chocolate, get to work putting my clothes away, and test out the pillow of decadent softness that is the bed.

I could live here forever. My word. I'd have paid five thousand dollars to stay in a room with nothing but this bed for twenty-four days.

Man, all this luxury seems shockingly sketchy considering what I paid for it. I seriously hope I vetted everything well enough. It would put a total damper on the first vacation I've had in years if these next few weeks turn into a sincere fight for survival.

Ha ha.

Yeah, that would suck.

❖

"*Valued guests of Gingerbread Inn, Jack Frost appears to have gotten carried away this evening. We would like to remind everyone that while this unexpected phenomenon fits perfectly with our story, we are incapable of actually controlling the weather. Although we advertise an 'open world' structure during the time we don't have events planned, we are—for your safety tonight—asking all participants to remain within the inn."*

I snort awake to the sound of Holly's voice rippling through the speakers. Turning, I run a hand through my long blond hair and freeze.

It's…snowing. In Florida.

Wind is whipping white streaks across the pitch black window next to me. Tumbling out of bed, I press my hands to the icy glass. My breath fogs between my fingers. Streetlights strung with flailing garlands illuminate patches of snow building beside the roads.

*"We repeat, this freak blizzard is not part of the game. We cannot control the weather. Stay inside. Do not require our staff to secure both you and the rescue animals that live in our village. We will prioritize the animals because you should know better."*

I laugh, and more fog coats the glass. This is incredible. It's a Christmapocalypse miracle.

*"Come tomorrow, once the threat has passed, we will absolutely pretend we planned this, but tonight stay. inside. In your rooms, even. It will help us out tremendously if we don't have to hunt anyone down. Thank you."*

The buzz cuts off, replaced by the soft Christmas music once more, and I stay right where I am, watching snow cut sideways across the wonderland scene.

It's beautiful. I've never seen anything like it.

Having never left Florida before, I've only ever seen snow in movies.

A blizzard in Florida.

Maybe it really is the apocalypse.

While I'm very invested in letting my poor fingers freeze as I watch it snow sideways, a bleak yellow light in the distance catches my attention. I watch it skid at an odd angle, streaking on the outskirts of the main cluster of buildings centered around Gingerbread Inn.

It takes me a long, hypnotized moment to realize the *light* is attached to a *vehicle*, and that *vehicle* is not entirely *on the road*.

My mouth falls open when the light vanishes. I can't see the car at all, but I swear a large tree over there just shuddered.

Oh dear.

I dart for the closet and grab the warmest coat I have, which isn't completely warm but does have a windbreaker built in. I throw it over my cream cable-knit sweater and pull the reindeer hat I brought in the event of a post-apocalyptic ugly sweater contest on with it. I fly down the two steps that section the bed area of the room off from the rest and throw my door open. The whole ride down the elevator my heart hammers in my chest.

I'm almost entirely certain I just saw a person hit a tree during a *blizzard* in Florida. We Floridians *do not* have a rule book for this.

The doors open on a fully-lit lobby *packed* with animals, and my mouth falls open.

A mutt turns toward me, honing in on the stranger, and barks, starting a cacophony of yips from the other residents sprawled across beds laid out amidst the disarray from before.

My stomach twists when the dozen or so elves look up, each and every one in full disconcerting costume. Over-green and much-too-vibrant red eyes pierce me, painted faces and extreme outfits fighting for my attention above the throngs of animals.

I don't know what all these actors and actresses have planned for this week, but I don't think anything can beat how eerie this moment feels.

"Mari!" Tessa snips, padding her way over as her elven companions set about calming the dogs. "Holly *just* told everyone to stay in their rooms." She cradles something in her arms, in a hat, and I look down to find a tiny, shivering kitten. "What's wrong?"

Nothing. Nothing at all. Oh my goodness. It's a kitten. Look at it. It's so small.

It yawns, and I clap my hand to my mouth to hold in the squeal that wants to break free.

Wait. No. Something is wrong. Very wrong.

I take a breath and move my attention off the tiny calico creature. "I was watching the snow outside my window, and I'm pretty sure I just saw a car crash into a tree on the outskirts of the village. I wasn't sure if I was the only one who saw it, and I figure it's better to mention it and risk having it mentioned more than once than it is to not mention it at all and potentially leave someone out there when they could be hurt."

Tessa's face pales, and she turns right as Jack comes up beside her. Worry eats up his electric blue eyes as he fixes his attention on me. "Are you willing to show me where if someone hasn't already found the crash?"

"Of course."

He nods once, lifting a hand to his ear, where I'm just now realizing a near-invisible earpiece rests. "Holly? Did you see any vehicles out there?"

Moments pass, and Jack's jaw tightens along with his fist.

After a moment his head shakes. "She's on the other side of the village securing more animals in the Candy Cane Cafe with the other elves." He turns on his heel and pulls a flashlight out of his coat. "Pepp, you're coming with us."

A burly man who looks like he's about to burst out of his elf uniform falls into place behind Jack. I glance one last time at the tiny kitten in Tessa's hands before I follow them both out into the beating wind. A curse explodes from my lips as I drag my reindeer hat down around my instantly frozen cheeks.

Jack's and Pepp's boots crunch through the thin layer of snow on the grass. "Stay off the street," Jack yells above the wind. "Chances are this person hit black ice. Test your steps in the grass before you commit to them."

My teeth chatter, but I manage something akin to a reply, pointing toward where I saw the crash as we leave the quaint heart of the apocalypse village behind. Squinting through the cloudy darkness, I call, "It was this way, dead ahead I'm pretty sure."

"I see the vehicle." Pepp's gruff voice blends into the screaming wind.

"I see the person," Jack adds, shining his light across the silhouette of a tall man blocking his face from the beat of snow with his arm. He trudges forward, steps cautious.

"Are you okay?" Jack yells.

"Yes!" the man calls, his voice ripped away by the torrent. In spite of the beating in my ears, something about that voice is so…familiar.

Painfully familiar.

My chest squeezes, and the burning breaths in my lungs stutter.

Like so much broken glass, fragments of my heart rain into my stomach. I force down an icy swallow as the man steps into the gleam of the flashlight and squints past his arm.

"Ryder," I whisper, all at once cold for reasons outside of the pouring sleet.

His honey-brown eyes lock on me, and he stills, every

muscle in his body going as tight as mine. His dark gaze slashes toward Jack, then to Pepp, and the seconds turn into hours.

No.

Of everyone in this whole entire world, it just has to be…*him*.

His lips form my name, too softly for me to hear, but just seeing them move in that ever familiar shape strikes me through the chest.

Ryder always called me *gold* when no one else ever has. He always knew how to make me feel as precious as gold, too, until he *stopped*. And we fell apart. He was my best friend growing up, the one stable person who kept showing up in my life as I existed in an over-crowded, ever-shifting system.

I gave him my heart.

He gave it up.

As a couple, we only lasted the second half of senior year, then we graduated, and we didn't fit together anymore —or so he said. By the next month, he was gone. Completely. And I never learned where he ended up.

But now he's *here*. In front of me. And I remember *everything* about him like he never left.

"—ri? Mari?" Jack touches my shoulder, shaking me slightly. "Are you okay? All of us need to get back inside."

Numbly, I nod, dropping my attention off Ryder until a weird sound rips into the storm.

It sounds almost like a *quack*.

# CHAPTER 3

♥ The duck's name is Jimmy. The man finds himself follicly-challenged.

I don't know how many shocking things are allowed to occur at the same time.

There's the fact I am seated on a couch that was only just recently turned right-side up because I'm at a roleplay vacation event called *Christmapocalypse*.

There's the fact I'm holding a tiny (emotional support) kitten in my lap.

There's the fact the man beside me used to be my best friend and is now my ex boyfriend.

There's the fact there are a dozen elves in this room taking care of several dozen dogs and cats.

But, honestly? All *those* facts hardly compare to—

Jimmy quacks.

Because *Jimmy* is a duck.

A duck who belongs to Ryder. A duck who is snuggled up in Ryder's coat.

Jimmy is a very happy white duck with a bright orange beak and little orange feet.

Jimmy is very small, like a toy duck, if toy ducks are a thing?

Jimmy is wearing a diaper.

The diaper has flowers on it. And it looks hand-sewn. And, no, I don't know how to feel about that, but, yes, I have already checked Ryder's left hand for a ring. It's the only conclusion I could come to when I saw *Ryder*

18

huddling a *duck* in his coat. Obviously, he's married to some sweet girl who has a pet duck. Except she isn't here.

Finally, there's one other thing I find shocking…

Cutting my gaze off both my kitten and the duck, I let it climb up Ryder's profile, across the sharp cut of his crisp dark facial hair, to the shining peak of his pale, bald head.

His eyes catch on mine, and I jump, dropping my attention back to my kitten. So small. So purry. So fuzzy. Because it's covered in hair.

Unlike someone's head.

"You look well, gold," Ryder says, his voice a melody I once knew by heart. Now, its deep timber is a distant song I'm latching onto with nostalgia, forgotten pieces of it coming back like gut punches. It makes me want to cry, and I'm trying desperately to keep it together. I may actually need a legit emotional support kitten.

My tongue trips all over itself, ready to blurt things it shouldn't. I swallow every thought in my head and shift my weight, pouring my energy into staring at my ESK. I whisper, "Thank you. You too."

If I'm honest, he does not look *well*. He looks sexy. *Really* sexy. Like I'm having a moment of sheer feminine panic over here because I can't look him in the eye *sexy*. Last time I saw him, he had a full head of hair and shaved his face. His father's receding hairline hadn't caught up to him yet. Clearly, when it did, he decided to embrace the fact, stop shaving his face, and start shaving his head.

And. It. Works.

Sooo well.

It fits his severe character so much better, if he still has a *severe character*. For all I know, he traded that in for a duck.

Is he still looking at me?

I glance away from my kitten to check, and *yep*. He

19

sure is.

My eyes ping-pong between his face and *Jimmy*, because I can't wrap my mind around how *Ryder* is sitting next to me with a sleepy duck in his arms, petting its little head with his thumb like he knows how to be sweet.

Ryder doesn't know how to be *sweet*. He knows how to be strict and seductive. Hot. Spice. If sweet and spice were on a spectrum, he'd be firmly at the end with the chili peppers.

Ryder is the love child of Scrooge and the Grinch *before* any character development. He hates things like joy and holidays (indiscriminately, the man doesn't even like his birthday). He can't stand sugar. He cannot be bothered to pet *puppies* when they are held in front of him. I *know* because I once planned a date for us to go to a pet store and I was the person holding a puppy in front of him.

He cringed.

AT. A. PUPPY.

And then he said, "Tongue," locked his hands in his pockets, and looked away.

I yank my attention off him and let a shallow breath through my tight lungs.

Five years is a lot of time for some people. Just because I've spent it alone in my little apartment, working constantly to fill the chasm in my chest does not mean that's what everyone else has done. Who knows? Maybe he found his *sunshine girl* and she turned him into a total cinnamon roll who…pets ducks named Jimmy.

Who the heck named his duck *Jimmy*?

Does he have a kid?

That thought makes me somewhat nauseous, and I wish I could remember anything other than the static flashbacks playing every memory I have of this man in excruciating detail. I know my Melanie Richards book has helpful tips for communicating. I need to recall how one escapes from a conversation and flees to one's room. I wish to eat every last snack in there. It is the only cure for my current mental state.

"It's been a while," Ryder notes, and the distance in this line and the last make me *ache* inside.

It's like we don't know each other at all, and maybe we don't anymore, but it still hurts more than I can bear.

I loved him once. He was my best friend. I want to believe I still know the same secret details about him that I once did. But he's holding a duck.

"It has been a while," I whisper, squeezing my kitten's soft paws. Itty bitty claws peek out, and the little baby yawns.

"How are you?" he asks, and I have to give him props for the small talk.

The Ryder I knew didn't *do* small talk. He didn't care how anyone was or had been. He spoke primarily in grunts or eye rolls. Sarcasm. Smug, half-smiles whenever he dared to smile at all. "Fine. How are you?"

He shifts uncomfortably. "...fine. Except for my wrecked car."

"Right. Yeah. That's not entirely *fine*, is it?"

"No, I don't think so."

I attempt to smile reassuringly; he doesn't attempt to smile at all. When the silence is penetrating, I say, "I'm glad you weren't hurt."

He sighs. "There's nothing around for miles, and with the holiday coming up, I don't know what I'm going to do." Casting a glance over the back of the couch at the elf animal rescue team, he winces as though they aren't perfectly adorable at the moment—not a smidge of *might turn you into candy* in them as they focus on more important things. "I take it this place isn't...normal."

"No, it's not." It's quite *un*normal, rather. To him, it's probably just another one of my silly and annoying little plans. Like going to a pet store for a date. I don't know why he ever agreed to go out with me in the first place.

From the start, we were starkly opposite creatures. My brooding-male-lead obsessed head was the only thing that tripped and fell into his coarse nature. I can't even remember him ever telling me he loved me. Not once. Not even as friends. Even though we knew each other for years.

The bell on the front door chimes, and both of us turn to look as Holly shakes snow from her curls and pinpoints us where we're sitting on the couch. A sigh plows through her, and she comments a few things to some of the elves before heading our way.

"Hon, what are you still doing down here? Santa's helpers can humanely take care of our unexpected guest, promise."

I clear my throat and touch my kitten's nose. "Um, we grew up together. We're…catching up." *Catching up* is not exactly what I'd call whatever it is we're doing, but anyway…

Holly's brows rise. "Oh?"

I nod.

Grinning, she claps her hands. "Well, that's fantastic news then! See, there's no way a tow truck is getting anywhere in this. Florida just doesn't know what to do with snow, period." She snorts. "It's basically *the apocalypse* out there. That said, every room here is full, and we don't have any extra staff rooms either, *but* one of our guests does happen to be flying solo in our best suite…"

My eyes bug, my heart pounding. What happened to her reassuring me that *Santa's elves could humanely take care of this situation*? She is *not* saying what I think she's saying. She isn't. There's no way. I—

22

"Since you two know each other, would you be comfortable sharing the room?"

My mouth falls open.

What?

Um. Excuse me. Hi, yes.

We're seated on a perfectly functional couch at this exact moment. I know it's not particularly *massive* enough to hold the skyscraper of a man beside me, but *sharing a bedroom* cannot be the logical conclusion here. We're not in a rom-com. We aren't. We're in a *post-apocalyptic Christmas story.* By all expectations, this doesn't even need to end with a happily ever after. We can *all* get turned into candy monsters before the twenty-fifth.

Heck, I'll even volunteer!

"I don't mind that," Ryder says, and my stomach flops.

My attention whips toward him.

Gaze just as intense as I remember, he melts me from the inside out. "I'd really appreciate it."

He— I— We—

Does he not remember that we have *never* shared a bed before? The closest we ever came was when I fell asleep beside him on his family's couch during a *documentary night*. NOTE: it was NOT a MOVIE NIGHT. Because RYDER EVAN does NOT watch *MOVIES*.

"It's settled then." Holly—who I suspect is actually one hundred percent mischief—rests her hands on her hips, right beside her gun. "Seeing as *'tis the season* and Marigold happens to be our only single guest, so long as you don't have anywhere pressing to be, you're welcome to stay and partner with her for the rest of our event. Tonight's been chaotic in a different way than we in Wintergreen facilitate, but our usual festivities will continue tomorrow, and they are best enjoyed in pairs."

Shame rises hot to my cheeks, crushing me into

23

someone smaller than my kitten. How lovely.

Now Ryder knows I'm all by myself at a weird retreat. While he went on to have a pet duck, I made nothing of myself.

With all the gruff distaste of a wood chipper, Ryder mutters, "Festivities?"

"It's a…Christmas escape," I offer softly.

"And you came to a Christmas escape alone?"

My eyes fill with tears, but I don't want to cry, not here, not with Santa's entire workshop behind me, not next to Ryder. He was always commenting on how I cry so easily. I hate the idea that nothing has changed for me while he's clearly had some major awakenings. All the same, when I close my eyes, two tears go skating down my cheeks to splash onto my lap right beside my kitten.

Gentle, warm fingers trace my chin, lifting my face, and in the next moment I'm looking past my damp lashes at Ryder. He curls a knuckle beneath one eye, then the other. "Come now, you haven't changed one bit."

Long-abandoned emotions spark and zip down my spine.

"This…thing…lasts through Christmas?" he asks.

My bottom lip trembles, but I manage a soft, "Yes."

"For all I know, I'll be stranded until after the holidays. Might as well make the most of it."

He can't mean that. Ryder doesn't look on any bright sides. Whenever I told him to, he said they hurt his eyes. His favorite days are overcast and drizzly. His favorite color is black. It's like I don't know him at all. "You want to participate in Christmas activities within a post-apocalyptic setting where people are being turned into candy?"

Ryder's brows knit, and he shoots a glance behind me, toward where I think Holly is still standing. When his gaze returns to me, his tone bottoms out. "I'm sorry. What?"

I lift a shoulder. "That's the premise. Santa Claus cracked because too many people were bad, so he's decided to purge everyone naughty from this world by turning them into candy. We're among the few who remain, and we have to show our Christmas cheer while surviving the collapse of society in order to avoid the same fate."

Ryder looks at me like I'm insane, but I'm literally just along for the ride. Whoever wrote this whole thing is the crazy one. They were probably given far simpler instructions, but they said, "You know what I'm going to do instead? That, but stupider."

Self-conscious, I murmur, "It's fun. I'm planning to join the elves on the dark side."

Ryder closes his eyes, and a muscle in his jaw jumps. "Of course you are…" Sighing, he relaxes back against the couch, taking his warm touch with him as he resumes petting sleepy Jimmy's head. "All right. I'm in. But if the dark side has cookies, I don't want them."

Holly laughs. "Of course *this* dark side has cookies. That's part of the whole *thing*."

"Great," Ryder grunts.

"Excellent," Holly chirps. "Why don't you three head up to your room and try to get some rest? It's been a more eventful evening than expected."

It certainly has.

Ryder stands, holding Jimmy close, and stretches his back. Every toned inch of his six-five build flexes within his long-sleeve shirt, and I have the sneaking suspicion I will not be getting much rest tonight at all.

Subsequently, my mood does not improve when my kitten is taken away…

25

# CHAPTER 4

♥ He's the grumpy; she's the sunshine. And unlike in
stories, those personalities clash…

---

"Wow." Ryder steps into my room, dark eyes huge as he takes in every detail. "This is…"

Much too bright. Much too sweet. Much too sparkly.

He doesn't give me an adjective. He just catches my gaze and says, "You must have really done well for yourself."

Clasping a hand to my arm, I look away. "It's a lot more reasonable than it looks."

"As if I'd believe a millionaire's definition of 'reasonable.'"

I make just over forty thousand a year. And two-thirds of it goes to rent. The only reason I could even afford to come here at all was because I don't do *anything*. Every extra penny goes into savings, and my savings has sat there, unused, for years.

I wanted to treat myself to something bright and fun.

I wanted to get over…

My gaze catches on his the second I glance at him, and my stomach drops. I don't know what I'm supposed to do. I don't know if I'm comfortable putting my pajamas on in front of him anymore. I don't think I'm comfortable around him at all. Seeing him again, after he abandoned me, makes every moment leading up to his leaving sting like a fresh wound.

It was always going to happen.

I have *never* been enough for *anyone*. It's why no one wanted me growing up. It's why I struggle to keep friends. Ryder would tell me I smiled too wide. He'd call my outlook on life *toxic positivity*. I just wanted to be happy.

I *just* wanted to be happy.

But even at that, I fail.

I scrub my cheek when I feel the tears fall *again*. Three times in one day. Marvelous. I just *love* that.

See? I can be sarcastic, too.

"I'm sorry." Ryder's voice is almost too soft for me to hear, and then I can't hear anything over the way my heart leaps when his arms come around me—easily.

Okay.

Maybe *not* exactly *easily*. He's kind of stiff, like he doesn't know what he's doing, but innocent affection like this was always on me before. He handled the…*other* kinds of affection, shall we say.

And he was quite good at it.

I cover my mouth and melt against his chest as a sob wracks through me. His arms adjust, and I fit. Have I ever *fit* here, like this, before? "Why?" I croak, the word wet. "Why did you throw me away like everyone else?"

"I…" He sighs. "I was hurting you."

I shove him back, looking at him through glassy eyes. "*What?*"

He averts his gaze toward where Jimmy is fast asleep at his feet, head flopped over against the floor. "I was hurting you. It was the last thing I wanted to do. So I left."

My mouth opens, but the words die on my tongue, and I can't force them out anymore. I *can't* say it hurt me *the most* when he left. I can't say that it still hurts me so much I think about him every day. I can't. I'm supposed to be *fine* by now. He obviously is. He has a *duck*. No emotionally destroyed man can raise a duck who, by all accounts,

27

appears chill with wearing a diaper.

It's just not a thing that occurs in this world.

What I finally manage to say is, "Explain."

"Explain?" A bitter hint laces his word, and I wince. He points at me, his expression pained. "There. That, right there."

"What?" I ask.

"You winced at the tone of my voice alone, gold. Every time I didn't take a more enthusiastic part in the things you loved, you felt a little more rejected, but you plowed ahead, pretending you weren't hurt. It got to a point where I couldn't watch it anymore. I was never going to be the person you needed me to be. So I, as delicately as I knew how, took myself out of the equation." His fists clench at his sides, and his tone grates, terribly hard. "It's what you do when you're in—"

"Don't you dare," I snap, raking in a shaking breath. "I've never heard you say that, not when we were best friends, not when we were together. I refuse to hear it now." My own hands close into fists as tears pour down my cheeks to splash onto the tile. The soft Christmas music around me strains, turning mutated and twangy in my skull. "*Leaving* is not what you do when you're *in love*, Ryder. You stay. You work it out. You compromise and come to an understanding." I slap a shaking fist against my chest. "I'd have done *anything*—"

His voice rises. "I know!"

I freeze.

He swipes his hand down his trim beard. "Gold, you think I don't know that? You *were* doing everything you could to accommodate me when I should have been the one accommodating you. Between us, I am not the bright thing who should be protected—you are. Especially during those few months we were together, I watched you dull yourself to fit with me, and I hated it. You tried so hard, and I was too immature to even be considerate of your efforts." A harsh breath fills him, and I've never heard his voice so rough when he whispers, "I want to try again."

My shattered heart splits into a million more slivered pieces.

He continues, "Isn't this kind of...like fate?"

I stare at him long enough for my open mouth to go dry. I stare at him, replaying those words over and over.

Try again.

Fate.

What a joke.

What an absolute joke.

I don't even know where he lives. I don't even know why he was driving past this place. *Try again*, he says, like he has any right. We don't live in one of my romance stories. This isn't the start of everything working out. I don't trust him anymore.

I'm terrified he'll leave me again, right after I fall back in love with every last part of him—even the ones that make me wince.

My head shakes, and every muscle in my body loosens, numb. "No." I swallow, trying to moisten my mouth. "I'm sorry, Ryder. No. I can't be with someone who thinks leaving is ever the answer."

"Gold—"

"I can't. All I have *ever* wanted is someone willing to stay with me, and maybe it hurt you to watch me try my very best to keep the person *I loved*—" My voice cracks. "—but you should have known better than to think someone willing to give up everything for you wouldn't be hurt more by you walking away. It could have taken us years to figure it out. Maybe, if you'd stayed, we already would have." Scrubbing tears from my cheeks, I turn toward the closet and get my pajamas out of the dresser. "I'll use the bathroom first. Maybe the snow will have melted come morning. And you can leave."

Because maybe some of his bitterness did rub off on me, I add a whispered, "You're good at it," before I tuck into the bathroom and close the door.

# CHAPTER 5

♥ In a small town, there are Hallmark vibes. But it's still
the apocalypse. Merging both was not hard at all.

---

As expected, I didn't sleep very well last night. Even
though I put my back to Ryder, I could *feel* him behind me
in the giant bed. I imagined him staring at me with those
pained, almost desperate eyes, and whenever I fell asleep, I
dreamed he loved me until I remembered he didn't and
woke up crying.

This morning, the snow hasn't melted. It's bitterly cold
outside. And the guests of Christmapocalypse have been
tasked with hunting down breakfast. I am wearing three
sweaters, my reindeer hat, and a coat, but my nose and
fingers are still sad, red things that want a warm meal.

"Maybe we should try the Candy Cane Cafe?" Ryder
suggests beside me, because until further notice *we are
partners*.

I've yet to decide whether or not being with him is
better than being alone. For all I know, he'll leave right
before Christmas, and I'll be stuck by myself while
everyone else who is paired up huddles together beneath
the light of the nuclear bombs. Or…whatever climatic
"Christmapocalypse" event is planned for "the big day."

Maybe Santa Claus will appear and turn us all into
candy no matter what we do. That's how most horror
games that give you hope end. The monster still gets you,
no matter how far or how fast you run.

I trudge through the snow in my sneakers, and the chill

wiggles its way through my socks to my toes. I don't know why Ryder has tall boots and a black trench coat, but I am jealous of him for looking so toasty.

Well, almost *so toasty*.

My gaze catches on his poor head. It is bare to the elements. I think it's a second away from frosting over.

"Did you hear me?" he asks, pulling my attention down to where Jimmy is peeking out of his coat, the most contented little duck in the world.

"Why wouldn't *everyone* have thought to go to the cafe? This is an apocalypse, and it's breakfast time. We'd have to fight to the death if we went to the most obvious place."

Ryder arches a disbelieving brow, maintaining his grumbly personality despite his *wanting to try again* last night.

I guess I'm just not worth fighting for.

I'm glad I made the right decision.

"Gold," he notes, almost *patiently*, "this is a Christmas thing. In a Hallmark village. You're staying in a room full of decorations and sweets. I highly *doubt* we're going to have to fight to the death over breakfast."

I lift my frozen nose in the air and keep wandering down the snow-padded lane, which does happen to be perfectly decorated with cheerful Christmas things. The buildings are also pristine, as though they were new right before the apocalypse and haven't had a chance to wear down yet. The interiors of some stores we've passed have been turned upside down like the inn lobby, but nothing appears noticeably broken, and everything is decorated.

Stalling some, I take in a window display in front of a clothing store that is dark but otherwise almost untouched. I stare at the reindeer in a ballgown surrounded by fake snow and cheerful lights. The eerie dark backdrop of the store clashes with it.

It's seriously like someone said *apocalypse, Christmas, Hallmark, smoosh* and rolled with it.

A cold breeze makes me shiver, so I stride toward the front door and reach for the handle.

"I doubt breakfast is in there," Ryder offers.

"I'm freezing. I didn't bring boots with me, because Florida, and my socks are wet." I try the handle, but it doesn't budge. Squinting, I locate rows of nice warm shoes and whimper. "I guess this is just a façade and we aren't supposed to go in there."

"Or it's realistic, and we're supposed to break the window."

Dully, I glare at him. "We are not going to break things."

His brows rise. "It's the apocalypse. We're *supposed* to break things."

"There is no way this event is sustainable if people come in and force them to change all their windows each time."

Ryder rolls his eyes. "I guess they really don't care about realism."

I fold my arms. "Ryder, I know you missed out on the first super fun initiation, but a man literally collapsed into a pile of candy. *Realism* was not the goal."

"Was humor? Because you see how that sounds like one big joke, don't you?"

I rest my forehead against the window door and feel the bite of the glass right through my hat. "We are going to starve and freeze to death. I can't believe I didn't survive one day during the apocalypse."

Ryder grumbles, "Pessimism has never suited you."

"Guess I'm falling back into old habits of making you comfortable." Yeesh. Five years alone has made me bitter.

It's easy to see where he had his reasons to leave. I guess I just wish he'd shared them with me so we could have tried to do better together. Too little, too late.

The me from several years ago would slap her cold hands against her cheeks and *make the most of this*, but the me right now is tired. I wanted to have a fun vacation where I attempted to move beyond the ghosts of my past. I wanted to heal and finally escape the lonely rut.

The last thing I wanted was to end up stuck in the very memories and moments that cut me to my soul. It's all going miraculously wrong. You don't get much practice being the *bubbly bright one* alone in an apartment for five years.

"I'll look for a back entrance," Ryder says.

"Why would a back entrance be any more open than the front one?" I ask, unmoved. My arms dangle in front of me, weightless and floppy. My hands are so very red. This is illegal. We're in Florida. It really is the apocalypse.

Ryder crunches to the alley. "For the sake of making the story more interesting? I don't know." Something clicks and creaks, whining into the cold air, and I straighten.

"What?" I peer around the corner to where Ryder is arching a brow at me and displaying the open door leading into the darkness.

"Ta da," he drones.

Frowning, I trot up to him and tuck out of the wind. It's warmer inside, for some reason. It's like the heat is on low. I am not going to complain about the momentary relief. "I'll go find some stuff," I say as Ryder steps in behind me and closes out the cold.

"I'll come with you."

"Why? You're perfectly warm." Except for his cold head. His poor, poor cold head.

He watches me, opting to cradle Jimmy's weight

against his other arm as he fidgets. Muttering, he says, "You used to like having me come with you clothes shopping."

My eyes roll as I wander from the back into the dim storefront packed with untouched clothes. It's not even dusty in here. Weird. "As I recall, you hated going with me."

"I didn't understand what the point was."

"I wanted you to tell me I was pretty, obviously." Scoffing, I head toward a basket of socks and start sifting through the thick, soft pairs. They are cozy and fuzzy, and I want thirty. I wasn't told there were any "hidden charges," so even though these are still packaged, it's fine, right? We're allowed to be anywhere in Wintergreen. That's part of the whole...*thing*. This is the free-roam Christmas Apocalypse village.

"You're pretty no matter what you wear. It's a unique torture to go with you and watch you change into a hundred different outfits, many of which required me to pretend I wasn't turned on every time you asked me to zip you up."

"*The point* was to turn you on, stupid," I comment, finally caving and deciding I'm going to use the socks whether it's allowed or not.

"That's abuse," Ryder tells me.

Eyes narrow, I rip the plastic linking the socks together and stare at him. "I'm sorry that I'm shy and had to find innocent ways to flirt with you. I'm sorry that it went over your head and you didn't take advantage of the situation."

Jimmy squirms, so Ryder undoes his coat to let him down, and he quacks as he wanders under a clothing rack. Ryder ignores where his duck is heading off to entirely and lifts a hand. "*I'm sorry.* I was supposed to know it was okay to *take advantage* of you?"

"Yes!"

35

He throws both his arms up. "Guys go to jail for stuff like that!"

I groan and head toward the boots, selecting a pair in my size that look sturdy—in case I need to run. Hello. It's the apocalypse. Something bad is going to happen right when I'm enjoying the Christmas part. *IT'S WHAT I SIGNED UP FOR.* I will not be in fancy thigh-highs for the occasion. "If I didn't like something, I would just tell you to stop."

"No," he states, voice hard. "You wouldn't have. Gold, you'd have given me anything I asked for if I suggested it might make me like you more. You've always done anything to feel wanted."

"Have I always been so…" My teeth grit as I try to find the word. "…spineless to you?"

He stares, jaw tight, and it's the most scalding answer possible.

"I see," I mutter, flopping down into a chair by the racks and struggling out of my soaked sneakers.

After I've just managed to get them off, Ryder drops to his knees in front of me and lifts one foot into his lap.

My breath catches, my heart squeezing. Compared to my iced feet, his cold hands feel almost warm as he strips off my wet socks. Keeping his voice low, he dries my skin with his sleeve. "I'm not going to lie to you, gold. Don't do me the injustice of lying to yourself. I spent most of our childhood protecting you from people who took advantage of your heart. I broke that one jerk's arm when he kissed you against your will in middle school, didn't I? Do you remember that?"

I shudder when he locks his eyes on me and slips the warm pink sock onto my foot. I whisper, "I remember."

"So you remember how you told me you pretended to like it before you found an excuse to get away then came to

36

me sobbing?"

I press my lips together, feeling tears brim in my eyes. Weakly, I say, "It was my first kiss. And he…he made it clear he just wanted to fool around. I…"

Ryder's gaze bores through me, and I can't hold it anymore.

I look away, clenching my jaw so hard it aches. "So I'm weak-willed and a shell of whatever person I'm around. Why did you *ever* bother going out with m—"

He squeezes my foot, enunciating very carefully, "*Because*, gold, I loved you."

My stomach hurts. My chest hurts. My body hurts. I can't breathe. I didn't want to hear that. I told him I didn't want to hear it. But he waited one measly day and said it anyway.

Gently, he pulls the other sock on and gets started removing the paper from each boot as he murmurs, "I still love you. I've always loved you. I've made a million mistakes, and I know I'm nothing like you, but I absolutely adore you, gold."

My throat closes as yet more tears threaten to spill over. My voice cracks, breaking, "*You left.*"

His voice rises. "I *did*. But if I'd known my leaving was going to steal your light just as much as my staying, I never would have. I couldn't bear watching myself destroy you. But it's clear I still—" He curses. "—it up." Pulling the boots on, he tugs the laces into a bow and growls, "You *have* to understand I messed up, but I sincerely thought I was doing what was best for you. I have wanted and missed you every day. No man in his right mind would *ever* give up a woman like you who is willing to do anything for him. Had I loved you less, I'd have been more selfish, and maybe then you'd still love me."

I *do* still love him. Obviously I still love him. If *I* loved

37

*him* less, this wouldn't hurt *so much.*

He cups my cheek, cold skin to cold skin. "My golden girl…" he whispers. "You are everything to me."

A tear falls to follow the line of his thumb to my chin. It drops onto my lap.

Letting his hand fall, he sighs and rests his head against my knees. "I want things to be different now. I want to do everything right, but I don't know how. All I can ask is for you to let us try again. If loving you can be enough—"

"It isn't," I whisper.

He tenses.

"This isn't a storybook, and I've gone too numb to allow others to define me now. Just loving me isn't enough. I'll accept that you sincerely thought you were doing what was best for me in the moment, but you have to understand there were other options. You picked the one that was the least work."

His head whips up. "*The least work?* It's been agony without you. I've wanted to come *home* every day. But I knew I couldn't do that to you until I had put in the work. I knew I had to do better before I could even entertain the idea of coming back into your life."

"I never told you to leave home," I snap. "You could have stayed. It was a big city. We never would have seen each other even if you hadn't disappeared without a trace."

"*You're* my home, Marigold," he growls. "*You.*" He takes a deep breath, letting it out slowly. When he speaks again, his tone is level, but it's no less rough. "I've spent these past years figuring myself out and working toward being the man you not only want but also deserve. I've worked toward becoming someone who can tell you *I love you* whenever you need to hear it, whenever you don't, whenever the compulsion overcomes me. I am wry humor and dry jokes. I am pessimism and sarcasm. But that was never the problem. Making you feel responsible for my negativity and never telling you how happy I was when I was with you, despite how I come off, was the problem. My happiest moments are a collage of you, and you needed to know it. You needed to know that you were worth just as much of my energy as you gave me of yours. I needed to show you that I loved going with you—anywhere and everywhere."

"Not clothes shopping," I whisper.

The touch of a smug smile lifts just one corner of his lips. "Clothes shopping is a unique case. I didn't entirely *not* enjoy it."

"I don't understand."

"Because you are innocent, and *clothes shopping* made me want to ruin that innocence with remarkable persuasion. But I couldn't do that. So it was blissful torture. I didn't like letting you know whenever you made me struggle to keep it together. Now I know better. You deserve to know how completely you destroy me."

My cheeks tint red for reasons outside of the cold. I drag my gaze off him and fold my arms.

He settles his chin on my knee, glancing up at me through his long, dark lashes. "Will you at least let me try to convince you I know how to treasure you properly now? Can we prove to each other that we are happy together without sacrificing any parts of ourselves?"

I don't know. I have no idea. But, more than anything, I think I want to try.

Slipping my reindeer hat off, I put it on his head and watch the softness in his expression mutate into something twitchy.

"Gold…"

"Your head looks cold," I tell him.

"It's a child's hat."

39

"It's adorable on you."

He crosses his arms beneath his chin and nestles them against my thighs as he sighs.

I never realized how deeply I missed the casual way he's always touched me, even platonically. He's garbage at initiating hugs, but this intimacy is something I think I've starved for every moment he's been gone.

"You're testing me. Is a reindeer hat the best you can do?"

"I think Christmapocalypse is the best I can do."

He arches a brow.

I grin. "Stay with me until Christmas."

"With you. In your bed." A flicker of his usual dry humor goes sparkling through his eye. "You still love to torture me, don't you?"

"Let's survive. If we survive until the end of this, okay. We'll give us another chance."

His brows jump, face seemingly going pale.

I frown. "What? You don't want to?"

"Of course I want to." He clears his throat. "It's just you don't know that we even *can* survive this thing. You don't know what the plot is. What if Santa appears at the end and turns us all into his candy monster thralls?"

"Then I guess I'll take a chance with *him*."

Ryder cringes, looking positively ill. "I know you have a 'thing' about villains, but…we're not talking about Loki or Jareth or…"

"Cardan, or Dark Heart, or the Darkling, or Wyre, or Jacks, or *Legend*, or absolutely any Hades."

Ryder's finger taps judgmentally against my thigh. Releasing a breath, he swipes his hand down his face. "I'm sorry. Back up. You said *Dark Heart*?"

"From *Care Bears*. My first love."

"That's what I thought and didn't want to believe." He

40

melts against me, croaking, "I need a moment."

A laugh bursts out of me.

He turns his cheek against his arms, glancing my way as a touch of warmth returns to his eyes. "There you are," he whispers.

I bite my lip in an effort to tame my smile. In this moment, it's impossible.

"It's cute how indiscriminate you are when it comes to your fictional boyfriends—seriously, not drawing the line at *homicide* is an absolute turn on. But, please, we're talking about an ancient guy in a red suit. Evil Santa Claus, gold. There's a line. This has to be the line."

"My track record with faeries and vampires says *age doesn't matter.* Also, have you seen *Guardians*? Jack Frost is obviously the best, but tough, tattooed Santa wasn't bad either. It's a whole weird genre this time of year to have stories with 'young and attractive' Santas who fall for their 'Mrs. Claus.'"

"Yeah, I'm genuinely scared what trouble you've gotten into without me."

I hum. "Best not leave ever again then, I guess."

"If that's permission to stalk you on the chance we both turn into candy monsters before Christmas, I'll take it."

Shrugging, I slip away from him and wander toward the coats in an effort to find something a little warmer than my three-sweater and windbreaker outfit. "I'm not really interested in stalker tropes."

Ryder clicks his tongue. "There's the line. How... reassuring."

I lift a large pink coat padded with a layer of down off the rack and throw him a lopsided grin.

He returns my smile gently, letting the expression rest more in his eyes than his mouth. I've missed that look. So much more than I knew.

It's too soon to hope. We still have an apocalypse to survive.

# CHAPTER 6

♥ Potatoes. Hot chocolate. And the apocalypse. I made it an apocalypse, guys. Stop saying this isn't what you expected.

---

After getting kitted out at the clothing store, I agree that it's no longer ideal "breakfast time," so we are less likely to end up mauled if we try to hunt down some food at the Candy Cane Cafe.

Unlike the clothing store, the cafe's welcoming windows aren't a façade, and chiming music boasts activity well before we've arrived. Just as I'm beginning to think that *maybe* making it difficult to find food was never a part of the whole "Christmapocalypse escape plan" (because that would be a little inhumane for twenty-four days), the man who turned into a candy monster yesterday pushes out the door.

I freeze, lurching back, and throw my arms out to block Ryder safely behind me.

Candy-cane-swirled eyes flick toward me, the man's face painted in rainbow shades of sprinkles and covered with gummy bears. He grins, and I'm sincerely shocked that his teeth are clean instead of, I don't know, oozing chocolate syrup or something.

"Well," Ryder notes, "that's disturbing. Is this a zombie story? I didn't think you liked zombie stories."

My heart rate attests to the fact I kind of do find zombie stories unsettling. "We don't know how it spreads," I hiss, throwing a look over my shoulder at Ryder.

Perfectly calm, Ryder pets Jimmy's head and half-smirks at me. "Um. Gold. Love. It *doesn't* spread. Not without your permission. We're playing a game, and you can't physically turn into candy."

I scowl, utterly ignoring the fact he just called me *love*. And I love it. I refuse to love it. "I know that, but we have to take it *seriously* or it's no fun."

The candy man takes half an unsteady step toward us, letting the Candy Cane Cafe door chime shut behind him before he sweeps into a bow, twists on his heel, and starts walking in the other direction, whistling—eerily—"Santa Claus Is Coming to Town."

That song is seriously so creepy.

I wait until the candy man turns a corner before I drop my arms and laugh. "Isn't this *cool*? I think it's cool. I think it's the coolest thing ever."

"Of course you do," Ryder murmurs, and when I find his half-smile I realize the partial ire I learned to expect from him is absent.

He's noticeably more…open. Gentle. I don't know exactly what it is.

Maybe he really did change in order to accommodate who I am.

Whatever the case may be, my cheeks heat, and I smile at my toes before cautiously approaching the cafe. Warmth fills the interior, the quaint slew of elegant tables and chairs filled with elves. As far as I can tell, there are only elves in there, not a single other guest. "Did we miss out on breakfast time?" I murmur.

Ryder grabs the handle, and the bell chimes.

"Welcome!" an elf woman standing behind the bar counter beams. Silver and gold tinsel threads through each of her long box braids, and she tosses them over her shoulder as she waves.

Ryder glances at me. "I think maybe we're still allowed inside."

Inching toward him, I peek around his sturdy body at the smiling woman. *Juliana*, her name tag declares in extravagant print. Hm. Most of the other elves don't even bother looking up at us. Considering the candy man we just saw was the one from *yesterday*, it's probably safe.

Probably.

I grin.

"Is it okay to bring my duck in here?" Ryder asks, pointing at Jimmy.

Juliana laughs, the light sound so magical and tittering. "Of course. A few cats are hanging out to keep warm, too. We just keep them all out of the kitchen."

Now that they've been mentioned, I locate several fuzzy bodies draped across laps or cuddled together in the corner booths. I have always wanted to go to a cat cafe.

"You think we'll survive?" Ryder whispers to me.

"*Maybe*."

Eyes rolling, he strides in and takes a seat at the corner booth, letting Jimmy down. The duck, shockingly, waddles his way around the circle cushion to the cat pile and joins it. The cats, as though unaware they are interacting with a discount chicken strip, purr louder and welcome their new member.

I ease myself into the other side of the booth, watching the fuzzy slinkys. "This is the weirdest thing I have ever seen."

"A man with gummy bears on his face just bowed to us."

I loosen my new scarf from around my neck and settle it into my lap. "Point taken."

Juliana approaches with chiming steps and sets a menu in front of each of us before she pulls out a notepad. "Can I start you two off with anything to drink?"

"Black coffee," Ryder says.

Juliana gasps, jutting a lip. "*Coffee?*"

Conversation stills, and elves all over the restaurant turn to look at us.

Ryder glances at them, then back to Juliana. "What?"

Juliana's expression twists, vacant and unblinking. "*Nice* people don't drink coffee."

Ryder's eye twitches, and he growls, "*What?*"

"Hot chocolate!" I slap the menu I haven't even looked at yet. "With marshmallows and whip cream for me. Is it possible for my friend to get an unsweetened hot chocolate?"

Juliana brightens up, laughing merrily as she looks my way. "*Unsweetened?* Your friend is funny." She gasps, holding slender fingers in front of her bright red lips. "Oh my. Does the poor dear suffer from that human aversion to sugar? How insensitive of me." Shaking her head, she tuts and scribbles our drinks on her pad. "Would you like a candy cane in yours?"

I gasp like a five-year-old. "May I?"

Juliana taps my nose, and I feel like a happy child. "*Of course.* I'll be right back, lovelies. Take your time looking over the menu."

The second she wanders off and all the other elves return to their business, Ryder leans across the table, hissing, "'Nice people don't drink coffee'? What does *that* mean?"

"I don't know. I'm not an elf." I skim the menu. Fried potato. Potato patty. Potato pancakes. Potato omelet. Potato toast. I press my lips together.

"What?" Ryder asks, dropping his gaze to my menu.

"It's entirely potato-themed."

He rocks back in his seat and picks up his menu.

Confusion floods his eyes, and he turns the lamented sheet over before whispering a curse. "What is this place?"

"I guess potatoes are all that is left at the end of the world."

He stares at me, eyes narrowed and incredulous. The reindeer hat makes everything about that baffled and disturbed way he's looking at me *so* much better. "Yes. Potatoes. And hot chocolate. And fourteen million different types of candies and pastries, if our room is any indication."

I scan my selection again, chipper. "I like potatoes."

Ryder pinches the bridge of his nose. "I know. They're your favorite, aren't they?"

"They are just so versatile. Just look at all the breakfast options you can get out of a potato. There are a hundred more ways for lunch and dinner. It is the perfect food. I'm not surprised it endured."

"You're only three percent Irish. I think you need to calm down."

"Me Irish blood may be wee, lad, but 'tis strong as a keg o' Guinness."

Ryder slips his fingers from his nose to his mouth and watches me for a long moment.

After I've decided on potato pancakes and toast, I meet his eyes. "What?"

He curses. "You're beautiful."

My heart skips a beat.

Juliana sets our hot chocolate down, startling my attention away from him. A touch of her brightness falters when she catches his eye, but she recovers quickly, and I don't blame her when I glance at the murder on Ryder's face.

I'm surprised she doesn't find a way to claim he's being naughty before she plucks her pad out again and fixes her attention on me. "What would you like?"

"The pancakes and toast, please."

"Maple, strawberry, or blueberry syrup? And would you like jam for your toast?"

My mouth falls open. This is the happiest place in the world. Forget the apocalypse and candy people! There's *strawberry* syrup. Closing my mouth, I whisper, "Strawberry, for both? Please?"

Juliana giggles. "You got it, sweetie." She turns her expectant gaze on Ryder.

Breath puffs out his nose. "Omelet."

"Any syrup with that?"

A muscle in his jaw tweaks. "It's an…omelet."

Neither her bright eyes nor her smile falters.

"No. Thanks. I've got that…" He clears his throat. "Sugar thing."

She shrugs. "Syrup isn't *sugar*, sugar."

"I assure you it is."

Taking our menus with a flourish, Juliana pouts. "Poor, sad human. Maybe Santa will fix you if you ask."

I glow. "So we *will* see Santa?"

Juliana's laughter chimes. "Aw. Does anyone ever *see* Santa?" She taps my nose again, and you know what? I am totally okay with it. "You'd have to become one of his little helpers first." With a swish of her bouncing candy-cane skirt, she whirls away, and I grin at Ryder.

"No," he states.

"Do you think if I ask, I can be an elf?"

"Absolutely not."

"But—"

"I highly doubt these nice people want you to overturn their entire storyline by joining the antagonists."

I flutter my lashes. "You're just scared I'll fall for Santa."

"*Scared* isn't the word. *Disturbed* that option is even a thought in your head…maybe."

I snicker and stir the candy cane in my hot chocolate before lifting it to my lips. "It's a thing. There are entire family movie series about it."

"The concern is not that it *is* a thing. It's whether or not it *should* be."

I break the sharp tip off my candy cane and point the rest at him as I roll the piece against my tongue. "No stalking, no cheating, no killing children. And, no, it's not *stalking* if you don't discriminate, so Santa is in the clear."

"The bar is so low." Before I know what's happening, Ryder clasps my hand, pulls my arm closer to him, and slips my candy cane into his mouth.

My entire mind breaks, my heart flipping in my chest as his dark eyes close. His nose scrunches when he releases me, and he mutters, "How can you stand that? You might as well eat raw sugar."

I accidentally swallow my not *entirely* raw sugar, and when the shard nearly takes out my larynx, I come to my senses. "Quit it. We're not *together* yet, and with the way you're acting, you're not going to survive three days, much less twenty-three more."

Ryder, the monster, threads his fingers beneath his chin and smiles at me. "Gold, are you saying I'm behaving poorly?"

"Don't…"

His eyes twinkle. "You're calling me *naughty*?"

I let my eyes close and touch my candy cane to my tongue, the very same candy cane that just touched *his* tongue. "I guess some things about you haven't changed."

"I did try to keep your favorite parts."

I sigh.

That he did.

# CHAPTER 7

♥ Jimmy steals the popcorn that has been strung for the Christmas tree. He is not allowed to eat it, though.

---

"What a shame!" Holly declares, pouting as she marches into the inn's mingling area. The fire in the massive hearth crackles, one huge sectional sofa facing it, and another behind it facing a screen TV playing *The Nightmare Before Christmas*.

My favorite Christmas movie.

Looking up from where I'm sitting with Ryder, a handful of cats and small dogs, and several other guests on the fireplace side of the room, I pause stringing popcorn for any of the near dozen Christmas trees taking up the vast space. It's been an incredible day so far—breakfast at the Candy Cane Cafe, mashed potato and salad lunch at St. Nick's Diner, garlic roasted potato dinner at Rudoph's, all while sightseeing around the village and building an army of tiny snowmen with a couple elves.

As expected, Ryder's energy is at negative three hundred, but he's still wearing my reindeer hat as he monitors Jimmy.

Jimmy would very much like to eat the popcorn.

Ducks, apparently, are not supposed to eat popcorn—something about it not being in their *natural diet* and therefore indigestible. Leave it to Ryder to turn up his nose at a puppy years ago and now be muttering, "Jimmy… Jimmy, no. Jimmy," for an hour.

"What's wrong?" one of the other women stringing

popcorn asks.

Holly's too-green eyes spark above a pitiful frown. "We've lost four people already."

"Jimmy." Ryder pulls his duck away from the popcorn bowl I'm using for the eightieth time, and Jimmy quacks in protest, his little orange feet battling to get him toward popcorn heaven—or the duck version of the River Styx. Now that I'm thinking about it, Ryder has his own clothes and food for Jimmy with him. He must have gotten everything from his car while I was asleep this morning.

Where was he packed to go before he ran into the apocalypse? His parents' house?

Wait a second. Did Holly just say we've *lost four people*?

Turning my attention to the woman, who I am completely sure is actually an elf despite the fact her curly auburn hair *conveniently* covers her ears while all the other elves have their ears on display, I find her touching a hand to her chest. "Quite apparently, a couple got into a nasty argument today—very naughty. And the partner of the man who was changed yesterday cried all night." Holly shakes her head. "They were not happy tears, which—of course—are the only acceptable ones for the season according to Santa."

When I cried in front of Jack Frost, he and Tessa only tried to cheer me up. When I cried in front of Holly, and if I'm right that she's playing as a very poorly-disguised elf masquerading as our guide, I didn't face any consequences either.

WHICH MEANS the *turning into candy thing*? Yeah, it's totally on a *by choice* basis.

I am absolutely allowed to join the dark side whenever I want!

Flicking my attention to Ryder, who is giving Jimmy a

51

forehead-to-forehead pep talk about how sometimes little ducks do not get everything they want, I mute my ever-present desire for mischief.

He's so precious. Was he always this precious? As far back as I can remember, I was drawn to him. He carries himself like a misunderstood villain, and silly me was obviously attracted to that. I have a feeling these pieces of him stayed hidden away beneath the coarse exterior, though. I can't picture the him I knew being like this.

I think I'll stick on this side of the tracks…just a little longer. Yeah.

He catches my eye, and everything about him goes still. My heart jumps, and I look away, feeling heat rise to my cheeks. I wish I could blame it on the massive fire crackling in front of us, but I can't.

Holly clasps her hands, imploring. "Ladies and gentlemen, *please* make sure you are showing your Christmas spirit and remaining in high spirits while you do. Jack Frost has already displayed his abilities, and—sometimes—he gets carried away."

A man asks, "What do you mean?"

Expression severe, Holly murmurs, "Being turned into candy is a blessing, Mark. Becoming one of Santa's minions is relatively painless after the process is complete, and though it *does* turn you insane, the best parts of who you are remain intact. When Jack Frost gets upset?" Holly pauses, allowing a frigid stillness to overcome the air, making it as stale as the popcorn we're stringing. "He turns people into ice puppets. And they are aware. And they are freezing."

Threads of fear ripple across the people around me before a hum of murmured conversation winds between them.

All I can think is *wow*, I know it's the apocalypse, but

that's freaking dark. Also, Jack Frost was super sweet with me.

Shoving off every bad vibe she just brought in, Holly beams. "So! In order to appease Jack, tomorrow we'll be having a snow sculpture contest in the inn's backyard. Every room that remains is a team. I do hope we'll not create any more disappointment."

"Jimmy!" Ryder blurts the second Holly turns.

Jimmy launches for the string I'm holding, rips it out of my hands, and *runs*.

Holly twirls on her heel, facing us all again, momentarily shocked.

A girl screams when Jimmy waddles past her ankles, a flailing string of popcorn behind him. Ryder lunges, and a popcorn bowl flies, dousing me and several others in kernels.

The commotion that is a grown man chasing a duck around Christmas trees and couches (to the tune of "This is Halloween," no less) draws the attention of *elves*.

Seriously, they fold out of the corners, peeking into the two large glass doorways. Over-bright eyes and unsmiling faces follow the activity with chilling silence.

I know it's just a *roleplay* but holy heck this is creepy. My stomach twists, so I do the only thing I can think of and laugh. Someone else joins in.

Then another person.

And another.

Soon, almost everyone on both massive couches is laughing.

"This isn't funny!" Ryder declares. "He's not supposed to have popcorn!"

Covering my smile, I locate Tessa among the curious elves, and her eyes catch on mine before she smiles and waves. I call, "You know how to take care of animals. Can you help?"

Bouncing on her heels, she throws one hand against her hip and lifts the other. "Obviously!" She snaps, and the half dozen elven witnesses alert, blank expressions filling with grins. Laughing, the elves filter into the room. In a matter of moments, they've got Jimmy cornered well enough he experiences a moment of ducky panic.

Ryder snatches him and pulls the popcorn string out of his mouth. Huffing, he spins Jimmy around and scowls. "We'll discuss this *later*."

Jimmy quacks, a squirming final protest, then the room erupts with fresh laughter.

# CHAPTER 8

♥ The date is winter-themed, and there are Christmas
lights. But also fire. Because apocalypse.

---

Sixteen days left until Christmas.

We've lost eight more pairs of people, and I can't help
but think it's strange that we've lost a couple each day
we've been here—like it's all planned. For instance, during
the snow sculpture contest, Jack Frost appeared and
declared a *loser* when we hadn't been told there would be
any ramifications for failing to mold sludge into something
recognizable.

Watching ice puppets drag the screaming team away
before he popped over to Ryder and I in order to
compliment our snow duck was…disturbing? I mean, not
nearly as disturbing as seeing them standing guard in front
of Rudolph's like empty, shuddering husks painted in icy
blues two days later…but anyway.

I've convinced myself that *maybe* not all the guests are
actually guests. It's the only thing—outside of *real* magic—
that makes sense. Some of the people acting as guests
aren't actually guests, and the people who are actually
paying guests will be the ones who "survive."

"It's probably all real," Ryder says, lying beside me in
bed after I've relayed my assumptions.

Sighing, I let my eyes roll before I turn to face him.
"Very funny. Weren't you telling me before that this was all
fake and I shouldn't be taking it so seriously?"

He faces me, and it hits me that we've been getting

along really well this past week, like old times, but... somehow better. Even with people getting turned into ice puppets and candy monsters, I have my best friend back in my life.

And I have missed him like air.

Ryder murmurs, "If I were running this kind of thing, I'd space out the actor guests who end up succumbing to whatever creepy magic is going on. Grouping them all into the first week will make the other weeks stale. Also, if I honestly do have so many actors playing as guests, where in the world am I making any money? You've already mentioned this whole thing isn't as expensive as it looks. Something weird has to be going on, because from a business standpoint, it fails to be sustainable. Therefore, Christmapocalypse magic."

He has some good points. But Christmas horror magic being real is absolutely not the answer. Why have I become the realist between us?

I whisper, as though elves are listening in, "What if the ice puppet guests are the actors, but the candy monster ones are real guests who have chosen to join the other side?"

Ryder's lips purse as his gaze wanders, and he gives his head a slight shake. "Maybe? But we've only seen the candy monsters briefly now and again after they've been turned. Who would agree to make themselves almost obsolete and give up taking part in the games? They're a big part of the selling point."

"You've always been so business-minded."

"Thank you."

I exhale a laugh, and for some reason I'm a little closer to him than I was before. This dangerous game of pretend apocalypse hardly compares to the dangerous game between us. I've missed him so much it's easy to forget he left when I needed him most. Every part of me wants to start again as though things never ended.

At some point while we've been apart, I think I kept some of him and he kept some of me.

Hence why it feels like we're arguing one another's views concerning this.

"It's not real magic," I say. "That doesn't exist."

"Of course it does. It just doesn't go by that fantasy name."

I hum. "Oh yeah?"

"Yeah." The corner of his mouth curls. "We call it love."

Groaning to subdue my laugh, I let my eyes roll yet again. "*Love* is turning people into candy?"

His honey-dark eyes twinkle. "It's the only explanation."

I laugh and reach to cup his cheek, smoothing my thumb down the soft bristles of his beard. "You've gotten ridiculous during these past years."

His fingers curl around my wrist, so he can stroke my pulse. "I've outgrown the compulsion to keep your feet firmly planted on the ground. I never knew how deeply I enjoyed watching you fly until I had to live without the caress of your wings."

Wow... Okay. Dang.

"Since when are you so romantic?" I whisper.

"Since I got smart enough to realize you deserve everything I am physically capable of giving you, and then so much more."

We're closer again. I'm not sure which of us moved in.

Ryder presses his lips to my palm and holds my gaze, the dimmed decoration lights speckled all over the room illuminating his gentle expression. "If you're scared the magic will come for you, don't be."

I shake my head. "I'm not scared pretend magic is

57

going to get me. But, let me guess, you're trying to be smooth and say you'll protect me?"

He runs the tip of his nose against my pulse, kissing. "Sorry, gold, I think we both know it's only a matter of time before I'm targeted. I'm useless to protect you here where *blissful joy* is the greatest weapon. The only reason I've lasted this long is because you're sweet enough for the both of us. Turning you into candy would thin the delicacy."

Oh, holy night…

My breath stammers, and, yeah, I remember now. Ryder never had to *try* to be smooth. He's always had the grace of the villains that you dance with. And I've always found myself lost to the charm. Even back when it hurt me…

Thing is? These past days? He hasn't hurt me at all. I'm not afraid of getting on his nerves. I've not been worried about muting myself to make space for him. In the middle of the apocalypse, in the middle of a world crafted to be like the ones I've always loved to read about, I feel entirely free.

And he's shown me, every single day, that me at my purest, truest form is exactly who he wants.

We fit together now, neither of us forcing or subduing anything.

I whisper, "You're distracting me from uncovering the mystery. If we don't figure out what's going on, we won't survive."

"So what you're saying is *it's not real* but we do still have to figure it out in order to *survive*?" He arches a judgy brow.

I wiggle closer, and our foreheads touch. "It's not real, but we have to treat it like it is real, because there's totally a plot afoot, and if we don't figure it out, we are absolutely going to die."

"There's a bonfire tomorrow night," Ryder whispers. "Do you think the candy people with marshmallows all over their faces are safe?"

I gasp. "Ryder, that is entirely morbid."

"I am the only innocent bystander in this whole fiasco. The rest of you, in one way or another, signed up for this mess. Therefore, who between us is *really* the morbid one?"

My lips press together. "I didn't know *all* the details when I reserved my spot."

"You didn't need any details. You took one look at *Christmas* and *apocalypse* and said 'sign me up.'"

I actually took four or five looks at *meet new people* and called to inquire about the details. Speaking of meeting new people, I really have made more connections with the elves than the other guests, even now that I'm not a "sad and solo" player anymore. Figures I'm still drawn to the bright, creepy, and magical side of this story. How very "me."

One thing I'm sure of is the fact I won't be alone on Christmas anymore. If the stream of events actually allowed me to follow *How to Not Be Alone on Christmas*'s more or less reasonable steps, Melanie Richards would be proud.

❖

You know what I never thought I'd—ever, in my entire life—think?

*That is one sexy man changing a duck diaper.*

Yeah.

But, hey, I mean, here we are?

Leaning against the wall, I wait by the door and watch Ryder sitting on the floor with Jimmy, changing his one pink and purple floral diaper out for another covered in daisies. Jimmy's so used to this that he's flopped on his back, long neck swung at a depressed angle. A practical sigh breathes through his fuzzy white chest as his orange feet stick in the air. He has given up.

And Ryder knows it.

He coos, "I know, I know. Life is so hard for a little duck," as he fits the pins in place to effectively secure the cloth.

I have never, in my life, seen anything more paternal, gentle, adorable, other adjectives that culminate in my being utterly smitten… Clearing my throat once Ryder frees Jimmy from the torture and lets him go merrily up into a tiny tail wiggle, I ask, "So…Jimmy."

Ryder stands with the old diaper and heads toward the bathroom, eyeing me briefly. "Yes…?"

"How, what, when, where, *why*?" I trail him into the bathroom, scrunching my nose as he goes through the process of cleaning the diaper enough for it to go in the laundry.

"Some of those questions don't exactly have clear answers?"

"Why do you have a Jimmy? You've hated animals as long as I've known you."

"No, I have hated *dogs* as long as you've known me."

"And cats," I remind him.

"Tongues and fur." His lip curls. "No, wait. *Liberal* tongues and *aggressive* fur. Jimmy has a tongue, but he does not lick people. He physically can't, which is amazing, and feathers are superior to fur. I don't even know why I have to explain that."

I rest in the archway, arms folded. "Okay…so…"

"I have a Jimmy because I like Jimmy."

Holding back my laugh, I grip my bicep and pull myself together. Lines I never thought I'd hear come out of Ryder's mouth… "Where did you get Jimmy?"

He finishes taking care of the diaper and hangs it over the designated diaper rack to dry before he washes his hands. "Would you believe I found him in an alleyway? At night? In the rain?"

"Mm, no."

"Pity. I did. Surprised you weren't there to see it."

I laugh. "And the true story?"

"I found an abandoned egg near a pond where I live. When I didn't see the mother for two days, I figured I could either incubate it myself and give it a good life, or risk waiting any longer and letting it die."

When in the world did *Ryder Evan* become the most endearing person to exist?

"And you named him?" I ask, just to make sure.

"Yep. Jimmy is a marvelous name. Short for Jimothy Johnson Evan." He wipes his hands on a towel. "Are we ready to go play with fire in the woods during the apocalypse?"

I push off the wall. "Um. *Always?*"

His eyes roll as he shakes his head, and he gets Jimmy situated comfortably in his coat before we head to the elevator and find Pepp in the hotel lobby.

The burly elf lifts his chin in an upward nod.

"Where is everyone else?" Ryder asks.

"Some have gone on ahead; some will go after. I'm making sure no one's sent on top of each other."

A giddy spark lights in my chest. "Is this a test of courage? Are we going to have to battle in the woods, or flee from attackers, or hide in makeshift bunkers on our way to the bonfire?"

Pepp's heavy brows lower over his eyes, and he shoots a look at Ryder before clearing his throat. "Uh…I don't think so. Sorry." He sniffs, rubbing his neck. "I'm a muscle elf. I don't really keep track of anything else that's going on." He frames his hands in front of himself. "*Pepp, move this box of coal. Pepp, grab that human for infection.* Et cetera."

Infection? I swallow, nudging back toward Ryder. "So the candy monster transformation is caused by infection?"

Pepp, helpfully, shrugs and throws his thumb over his shoulder, directed at the door. "You two can go."

I adjust my scarf and try to smile. "Well, thank you."

The second we're outside, I realize I might be a little overdressed. The freak Florida snow has long-since melted away, leaving behind a slash of warm weather that makes my scarf somewhat obsolete. It also makes coddling Jimmy unnecessary.

Ryder sets him down as I open my new winter coat. "Will Jimmy be okay with the dogs wandering around? It's warm enough I bet all the rescue animals are back to free-roaming."

"He doesn't go far," Ryder says, and it's true. He's waddling after Ryder like Ryder is mother.

Ryder is totally mother.

And if I weren't so utterly convinced of that fact, I'd be more nervous. All things considered, I highly doubt Ryder —Mr. I change my duck's diaper five times a day—Evan is going to do anything that would put his feather child at risk.

"I think it's that way," he comments, pointing out across the field that separates the village from the woods. Near where his car remains sad and crunched, the forest glows. A trail of large lit candy canes sticking out of the grass loosely mark the path, and we follow them toward a growing trickle of music.

Subconsciously, I inch near Ryder and wait for the lights to flicker or the music to turn tinny.

"Scared?" he asks when my side bumps into him. He splays his hand for me, and it's been years since I've held his hand.

My fingers meld perfectly with his, and the touch is like a sigh. "We've just been told that the elves are *purposely* infecting people in order to turn them into candy monsters."

Ryder grunts, "And? That's new information?"

"Of course. It was just somewhat morbid magical whimsy before. *Now* it's creepy needles and stuff. Or bites."

"We've seen the candy people around. They look insane but otherwise not interested in biting people. If you're convinced this isn't real, I don't think they're allowed to bite."

I pout. "You're not exploring the terrifying possibilities with me."

Ryder's lips tug into a wry smirk as we march across the brittle lawn. "Okay. Terrifying possibility—the treats in your room are filled with infection serum, and you've been enjoying them for over a week. Maybe I *will* be the only one to survive this."

Crushing his hand in my fist, I am *immensely* grateful this is all pretend because, yikes, that's a valid concern if something like *infection serum* were a real thing. Of course the bright display of treats that has been cared for *daily* while we're out and about is a trap.

Goodness. I should know better.

"That's much too obvious, don't you think? Everyone would have already changed if that were the case."

"Maybe it only activates if you're naughty." He drags the back of my hand up to his mouth and catches my eye. "Something *you* will never be."

I bite my lip to tame my smile as warmth flushes into my cheeks. "When the first person turned, we had all just gotten here. No one had eaten anything, and nothing suspicious happened. He just collapsed."

"Interesting," Ryder murmurs against my knuckles. "Maybe that was an oversight in the storyline? Or *maybe* it is magic, and that guy mentioning *infection* was carefully-placed misdirection."

Shaking my head, I glance away from him and find myself standing at the treeline.

Breath leaves me.

Overhead, lights string across the boughs, dancing in time with the soft music flooding through the woods. Colorful bulbs coil around every single tree in front of me, lining the blinding path. White and blue fall like lit snow in streams.

My lips part.

Reindeer leading Santa's sleigh gleam in a sequence of lights that make it look like they're flying through the woods.

"Wow," I exhale.

Stillness consumes me, the morbid nature of this entire adventure forgotten for precious seconds. I understand it would be so easy to have everything before me turn static before it dies and plunges us into horrifying darkness…but that would be such a waste.

"All I Want for Christmas Is You" starts playing, and my heart leaps.

"It's my…" I begin.

"Favorite," Ryder finishes.

I turn to him, and everything in me shivers.

Illuminated by the lights, he's smiling at me. It's the softest look I've ever seen on his face. Sighing, he shakes his head, and his low voice melds into the tune as he begins to hum along. His fingers slip into my other hand, and he touches his forehead to mine.

I startle back. My hands slip free from his grip.

"What?" he murmurs.

He left me.

My heart's pounding, and I can't breathe.

He left me.

He left me, and he *didn't* come back. Fate is only beautiful in stories. In real life, it's an excuse. I would have preferred him to come back to me on his own, to *choose* me without destiny getting in the way.

It's so hard to remember that I don't know if this is safe, if it will *ever* be safe. He left me after we grew up together. No amount of time going forward will ever be enough. I'll always be scared of the chance he's capable of doing it again.

He destroyed me.

And it's easier to pretend that part didn't happen when we're acting like friends in this game. It's so much harder when he's looking at me like this in a wonderland that feels more like *romance* than *apocalypse*.

Ryder extends his hand, glowing in the darkness of this magical scene. His long, fitted coat flails around him in a sudden breeze, and he looks exactly like my every dark fantasy. "Come here, love."

"I shouldn't."

"Why?"

I clutch my fists against my chest and feel my heart pound in my skull. "You know why." Tears brim, and I've been doing so well to keep them under control. I've been doing so well to let myself get caught up in the magic and fantasy. For the first time in years, I haven't been lonely. "What if we're just supposed to be friends?" I ask. "We can be friends. Everything goes wrong when we complicate that. We lasted *years* as friends. And only months as lovers."

Ryder's smile drifts away, and he lowers his gaze but not his hand. "I messed up doing the wrong thing for the right reason. You love that."

"In books. Not real life."

His eyes close. "There was a time when you didn't want to differentiate. That's why you're here, isn't it? You wanted to live in a story."

"I outgrew believing that it was possible. I've spent my entire life waiting for my turn." A tear trails down my cheek. "In the real world, not every orphan gets to be the star of a story. Some of us don't even find our families. It's *so hard* to grow up being constantly reminded that no one wanted you." It hurts to swallow past the lump in my throat. "We haven't survived yet. And even if we do, I'll still be scared. Maybe I'll always be scared that you'll decide it's not worth watching me be afraid and leave me again."

"Never." Ryder's hand closes into a fist as his dark eyes flash open. "Never again, gold. No matter what happens or how you react, I can't live without you anymore." He takes a step toward me, opening his hand again in the slim space between us. Looking down into my eyes, he whispers, "Every second of every day we've been apart, I've been thinking about you. I would do anything for you, even set this whole world on fire. We are drastic opposites. But if *Christmapocalypse* somehow works, I think we should be able to as well." His breath falls across my lips as he leans in, and I feel the heat against my damp cheeks. "Brand me as yours, gold. I will prove to you the lengths I am willing to go to make you mine."

My fingers come apart, hesitant. He's trapped me in the burn of his gaze, and I can't look away. One fragile inch at a time, I reach for his hand.

He closes the final inch himself and clasps, binding us together before kissing my cheek. "All I want is you. Today. Tomorrow. For Christmas. For always."

And all I want is for him to *stay*.

# CHAPTER 9

♥ They went swimming in winter in Florida. But it was northern Florida and not the beach, so it was a bad idea.

---

Last night still has me in a daze. Not because of the bonfire. Or the fact candy monsters covered in marshmallows were the very people passing them out. Or because I ate enough cookies and drank enough hot chocolate to put me in a sugar coma.

No, the part of last night that leaves me ruined is everything that happened *before* Ryder led me through the mythical forest to the giant blaze surrounded by tables packed with trays of cookies and dispensers filled with hot chocolate.

Everything that came after that moment in the woods was my ditch effort at sorting my thoughts and keeping from breaking down in tears in front of everyone.

I want to survive this thing. Both of the *things*, rather. The apocalypse and my messed up emotions in regards to Ryder. Even though we're still losing pairs of people each day, the whole Ryder thing seems way more pressing. Because, you know, that part's real.

I'd be more concerned about us *losing people* if they were actually disappearing instead of just wandering around in new roles with new costumes. It's a little freaky, but not scary in a "I'm in actual danger" way. The trickle of unease stems from the fact it really is starting to feel like a poor business model.

If everyone who has been turned *isn't* an actor, why are

they so good at their new roles? I can't shake the feeling that something *real* and *freaky* is going on, but I don't feel weird like I've been drugged or anything. Potatoes for every meal and unlimited sweet snacks throughout is my definition of a good time. If I were drugged, I'd be entirely useless by now.

At the very least, whatever weirdness is going on doesn't seem malicious toward me in particular. From the first moment when Jack Frost and Tessa comforted me in the inn lobby it felt like I was on the side of the people who are in control.

The bed bounces, and my heart jerks out of my body as Ryder's face appears over me.

"What's wrong?" he asks.

Breathless, I say, "Huh?"

"You have been lying here for an hour." He casually combs his fingers through my hair and pins the long blond strands behind my ear.

Fighting the rush of heat rising to my cheeks, I look askance. "It's a free day without any special events, so I am attempting to unravel the mysteries."

"Can you unravel them outside?"

"Why would I want to do that?"

He lets his fingertip skim over my cheekbone. "Because, it's a relatively warm day, and Jimmy wants to go swimming. We passed a pond last night in the woods, and you may not have noticed, but he looked quite longingly that way…"

I noticed very little outside of Ryder last night, and I'm surprised he could see anything beyond the lights. The world past where they flooded was absolute pitch.

His finger moves to my lips, and I push him away, glancing up.

His hand closes into a fist that he places in his lap. "I'm

trying to cheer you up."

"Your efforts are appreciated."

"I'm not good at this sort of thing."

"Effort is more than enough, Ryder."

He cocks his head. "So you'll come with us?"

I roll upright with a dramatic sigh and smile. "As if I can let you go anywhere by yourself. Your resting frowny face will land you on the naughty list for sure."

"Will it now?" His gaze warms as he helps me out of bed, and it takes every last bit of my willpower to keep my head on straight.

It's no secret that I want him. I have wanted him forever. But wanting him is like wanting a holiday. It comes; it passes; you realize it was never something you could hold, no matter how much you love it.

At some point, the magic disappears entirely, and it's just another day where you're trying to reach for the feeling it once gave you.

Ryder lifts a bathing suit out of the closet, and my brain shuts down.

"What?" I breathe, staring at the bikini. "Where did you…"

"The clothing store," he notes, perfectly casual. "Where do you think I've been this morning while you've been lying in here, staring at the ceiling?"

First of all, I was staring at the pretty canopy. Second of all… I bite my lip and look at the bikini. It's an actual bikini. In my size, no less. The asymmetrical red skirt that ties at the hip offers some modesty, but the rest? The rest is pretty much underwear. "You've been shopping for a bathing suit for me?"

"Shopping is a loose term, considering it's the apocalypse, and everything is free."

"Already paid for, technically." I take the hanger when

he offers it, and I'm sincerely wondering if I was under-charged. Maybe it was supposed to be thirty thousand dollars. I hope I have a legal leg to stand on if that discrepancy comes up. Three thousand is a chunk of my savings. Thirty thousand is money I don't have. "I'm surprised you survived." Skeptical, I shoot Ryder a glare. "You didn't laugh in some poor elf's face when they said you were put on the naughty list, right?"

"I can't believe you're siding with the *poor elves* who are dragging people away against their will."

"That would be illegal."

"Welcome to the apocalypse."

I guess Ryder is still on his "this is real" stint. It's kind of...cute. Yeah. Cute. Endearing too. Him no longer wanting to ruin these kinds of things for me by bringing in heaping helpings of realism is impossibly sweet. Coming from a man who would pick out unrealistic twists in his documentaries and note how certain things *couldn't have happened and must have been changed for dramatic effect...*

This openness toward something highly unrealistic and wonderfully silly is huge.

Why couldn't we have been like this before he irreparably changed everything I'll ever be able to see about him?

Taking a deep breath, I turn toward the bathroom. "Are you sure it's safe to go swimming during the apocalypse? What if the water is polluted by radiation?"

"It's not a radiation apocalypse. It's a candy magic one. Facilitated by Santa and elves, who want everything to be happy and perfect."

I blink over my shoulder at him. "What about bacteria in standing water? You said it was a pond."

"I'm sure there's an outlet. At the very least, Jimmy can

71

enjoy it."

I cut a glance at Jimmy, on Jimmy's bed, which is a small dog bed at the height of dog bed luxury. The padded light blue cushions sincerely have a claw-footed stand. It's still crazy to me that Ryder domesticated a duck of all things.

"It's not naughty to go swimming," Ryder tells me, the corner of his lips pulled up in a crooked smirk. "It's not like we're skinny dipping."

My cheeks heat, but with that I march myself into the bathroom and change.

❖

What do you know? There is a creek that feeds into the pond before continuing in a snaking path through the trees toward an adorable vacant cabin that I want to live in. Sunlight shines through the canopy to glisten across the water, and ripples skate over the surface in glinting sparks only Jimmy is presently disturbing as he darts around and dips his head beneath the surface.

I shoot a glance at Ryder and still.

Beside him, on a rock, is Jimmy's diaper bag— otherwise known as what Ryder was handling the last time I shot him a look. He is more than done with putting Jimmy's diaper away. *Now* he's dropped his jeans to reveal a forest green pair of bathing suit shorts and he's in the process of pulling off his shirt.

Arms I hadn't realized I'd folded unravel slowly to fall at my sides.

The fabric comes off completely, revealing toned, tan flesh. Strong muscles. Defined abs. Either he got more ripped these past few years, or absence has sweetened the wine.

He folds up his shirt to set it atop his jeans like he hasn't increased my body temperature by four thousand.

Then he catches me staring.

Our eyes lock, and I watch that dark gaze of his skim across *my* curves. Not an inch of my body is toned or defined like his. I'm all soft swells, and currently I'm spilling out of this fire-red bathing suit he picked for me.

The look he gives me in the silence of this moment broken only by a happy, splashy ducky translates roughly into *I'd be a fool to ever leave you.*

And he's right. He was a fool.

He was the fool, but now we both have to pay for it.

Pushing my hair back, I step carefully toward the rocks paving the creek outlet and dipping into a depression that seems like the easiest place to descend into the pond. The chilled water sends a shiver up my spine as I wade up to my calves. "It's cold."

Ryder leaps in, sending a frozen spray across my bared stomach. Every nerve in my body implodes.

"*Ryder!*" I swing my arms around myself, eyes wide on him as he surfaces and tosses droplets off his face. Jimmy quacks, rushing toward him to rub his little white head against his bicep. Sunlight hits them both, and Ryder laughs. "Okay, okay, yes. I love you, too. We're both in the water, and everything is amazing."

I have never seen something more precious in all my life.

Ryder throws off a shudder and pulls his gaze toward me. "Come here, love. It's not so bad once you're submerged." This time when he extends his hand, I fade into the chilled water in order to reach it without hesitation. He's a siren, calling me toward things I shouldn't trust. Or maybe they are things I wish I *could* trust. Broken trust is the hardest thing in the world to mend.

No matter how perfectly I fit beside him. Or how gentle he's capable of being. Or how entrancing the sound of his laughter is.

"It's still cold," I complain softly. "You could have gotten a heart attack."

"Hm?" Ryder pinches my chin, tipping my face up to meet his eyes. "What? When I looked at you in this?"

I turn my face out of his grasp, but since he's like a heater in this chilly pond, I lay my cheek against his shoulder. "You're impossible."

His arms coil around me, and *this*, right here and now, is the safest thing in the world. Or…I want it to be. Or it once was, and I'm desperate to get back to those moments.

"Gold, I—"

"No, please," I whisper, letting myself hold him. "I don't know what to think right now, Ryder. I don't know how to love in fragments. I don't know how to wrap my head around the fact you left me because I was trying my best to show I loved you, even at the expense of myself." I cling to every warm piece of him and close my eyes. "Please, for now while you're allowing it, let me pretend."

"I always should have allowed you to pretend whenever you were excited about pretending." He keeps me near as a fragile breath fills his chest. "I never should have made you feel like making me happy meant sacrificing any beautiful pieces of you. I was insecure and scared I'd lose you to your other loves. I was scared I couldn't measure up to the stories that excited you. In my head somehow I convinced myself I had to keep you grounded because that's where I was, and that hurt you, so I convinced myself we couldn't work, that you'd be happier with someone else. I was wrong. I have been so wrong."

"Please, Ryder. I need time."

A moment of icy pause fills the cracks between us, then he whispers, "Of course."

Forcing myself, I pull out of his arms and manage a

lopsided grin. "If we don't move around, we're going to freeze to death. Jimmy's got the right idea." I cut a glance at the duck zipping around us. Oh, to be a Jimmy, cheerfully playing in the water. The life of a pampered duck.

Without warning, Ryder splashes me, and the wave douses my entire head.

I gasp, shuddering. "What—"

He launches away from me, and *okay* I see how it is.

"Get back here!" I dart after him, throwing water. I might be shorter and standing on my tiptoes in the rock bed, but I will *not* lose in a water fight. It's practice for the inevitable apocalypse war set to occur on Christmas Eve. Obviously.

By the time we pull ourselves out of the battle, I'm shivering and laughing. Jimmy is content. And Ryder's almost-smile has stayed fixed on his lips nearly the entire time. He wraps me in a towel before getting a smaller one out for Jimmy, cleaning up his little footsies, and putting a fresh diaper on. The whole ordeal takes five precious minutes, and during them, I decide I want this.

The only issue is: I'm scared I'll never know how to keep it.

# CHAPTER 10

♥ There is a plot. In this *swamp* of unbalanced book suggestions squatteth a functional storyline.

The next few days pass in a blur, for I am ill.

The morning after our dalliance in the woods at the pond, I awoke with an awful headache. I could barely get up. And Ryder panicked when I almost fell out of bed. I slept off and on throughout the day, aware only that he never quite seemed to leave my side.

The headache and lightheadedness evolved into congestion and a cough after that, and let's just say *maybe* going swimming in winter can end horribly even in Florida. My brain must have relapsed. We are clearly in climates capable of producing a freak snowstorm. What made me think it would be warm enough to *swim*?

Potato soup is wonderful, though.

Ryder is really good at taking care of me, too.

I hope I'm not missing too much of the fun.

Does getting sick count as being naughty?

If a battle to the death happens while I feel this messed up, there's no way I'll survive.

Cold fingers touch my cheek, and I shiver as I crack my eyes open on icy blue skin.

Huh?

"Yikes." Jack Frost pulls his hand back like I've scalded his fingers. "Poor little human. I'll just cool you down a bit…" He lifts a finger, swirling it twice before Tessa bursts forward and grabs his hand.

76

She hisses, "Jack, you can't make it snow in here. Humans are weird, and when they get sick, they can't get too hot *or* too cold."

Jack sighs, rolling his frigid eyes away from Tessa. "If the boss didn't have plans for her, she'd be so much happier as a candy monster. *They* don't get sick."

"Wh…" I whisper. Why are they in my room? That's an invasion of privacy. There have to be rules against it. I drag my attention off them, trying to find Ryder.

"Sh, sh, sh," Tessa murmurs, shoving Jack aside and lifting a washcloth off my forehead. She dips it into a basin of water at my bedside, wrings it out, and puts it back. "Everything is *fine*, Mari."

Jack Frost strides to the other side of the room, and I drowsily look between them.

This is definitely weird.

Why would actors be in my room while I'm sick? I'm in my pajamas. That doesn't seem quite right?

"Tess," Jack calls, tossing a small box between his hands.

"Hm?" Tessa throws a look over her shoulder at him. "What?"

Jack laughs. "She hasn't opened any of her gifts. Do you think the boss is offended?"

"Uh. *Yeah?*" Tessa leaves my side, plants her hands at her hips, and huffs. "Goodness. No wonder he's been irritable lately. How terribly naughty of you, Mari."

I try to push myself upright, but my head spins, and I squeeze my eyes shut. "I'm sorry," I whisper. "I didn't know I was supposed to. I thought they were decorations."

Tessa gasps, setting a hand to her heart. "*Aw,* how terribly nice!"

I cough, and the next thing I know Tessa is at my side again, stroking my hair away from my damp brow.

"Don't worry," she practically coos. "Christmas is coming sooner than you think. The boss will take good care of you."

I squint. "What does…that mean?"

Her too-bright red eyes flash. "Christmas magic has to come from somewhere, and with so few people left in our little village, someone has to fuel next year's…sweetness."

My stomach tightens.

Jack smiles, the expression chilling. "*Don't worry.* He'll take good care of you."

The door opens, and Ryder marches in. "I'm sorry, gold." He ignores the two elves entirely, and they dance out of his way, laughing eerily. He begins setting things down on the table beside me. Medicine. A thermometer. Vitamin C.

"What…" I glance at the elves, and their smiles stretch behind Ryder. "The… Jack Frost."

Ryder looks at me, brows furrowed. "What?"

My eyes fix on him, and I squeeze them shut for a moment. When I open them again, the elves are gone. I didn't hear the door open or shut again.

I must be hallucinating.

Am I really *that* sick?

Ryder cups my cheek, and his hand is cool, but it's starkly different from the burning ice of Jack's hand. Can you hallucinate feeling something? "It's okay," Ryder murmurs. "I was able to find some things in one of the resident buildings on the edge of the village." His shaky smile makes my chest feel almost hollow. "It's getting pretty bad out there. But it'll be fine once you're well again." He takes my washcloth and kisses my forehead before genuine confusion knits his brow. "It's still fresh?" He looks between it and the bowl, shakes his head, and puts it back before he gets started opening the vitamin C.

I must be dreaming.

This is just a really strange dream.

Yeah.

"Ryder," I whisper, and he looks at me. My eyes close. "I love you. So much. I've never… I'll never…"

"Shh…" He caresses the backs of his fingers down my cheek. "It's okay."

"I'll never recover."

"Nonsense. It's a bad cold because someone was stupid and invited you to go swimming. I can hardly believe Jimmy's irresponsibility."

Where is Jimmy? In his bed? Did Ryder leave him here when he left to get this stuff?

"No." My head's a foggy mess. "From you leaving." I manage to swallow; it hurts so much. "I never got over it. I've been so scared, so lonely. You're my best friend. I love you."

Ryder kisses my cheek, his breath cool and lingering. "*I love you*, Marigold. I am so sorry. I'll show you. I promise. Somehow, we'll get through this, and I'll show you that you're everything to me. You'll be safe and happy again. I promise." He kisses my chin. "I promise."

I think I fall asleep.

My recovery is slow, so slow, but by the time I'm starting to feel better, I only know one thing—Ryder took care of me the entire time. And I might just be starting to believe him.

Nothing is scarier than that, except, maybe, the apocalypse.

❖

Five days till Christmas.

I can't believe my sickness knocked me out for so long, but perhaps what I can believe even less is the fact there are only ten of us left. Five pairs, including Ryder and I.

Everyone else has been turned to ice or candy, and they're either wandering like sentries around the village or languishing in insanity.

Among the other guests, unease runs rampant.

It's like I've woken up from my cold in a different world entirely.

Yesterday when I finally left my room, a few of the other humans thought I'd been *taken*. Most of my interactions have been with the elves, so I've not been directly included in many *human conversations*, but I have overheard a few things since rejoining the world of the living.

Things like *I asked Holly if I could go home, but she just laughed.*

Things like *I think Holly is one of them.*

Which, I mean, that part was pretty obvious, right? But since when are we concerned about it? *Them* are just people in costumes.

"It's definitely pretend, right?" I ask Ryder as we're getting ready to head toward Rudolph's, where a Christmas cookie contest is taking place today.

A cold front swept back in, bringing a chill with it while graciously leaving snow behind, so Ryder's pulling my reindeer hat on when he looks over his shoulder at me. He stares for an unsettling moment, and I can't shake the feeling he's been more quiet than usual ever since I got better.

"I'm not joking," I state. "I need you to tell me it's all just pretend, because you're good at being my voice of reason. You always have been."

Ryder, with Jimmy on his heels, strides toward me and fixes my scarf loosely around my neck. "Gold…while you were sick, I was exempt from everything going on here so I could take care of you, but I still saw and overheard things.

There's no way this is a business. There are only ten of us left, and I'm not supposed to be here. Nine normal people could never afford to make this anything sustainable."

I shake my head, laughing. "Come on, Ryder. We already decided that some of the candy monsters were—"

"There's no way. They've hardly been included in any activities. There's no way they paid to become part of the staff, gold."

I take a deep breath, scowling. "During the storm, Holly announced over the speakers that everyone was supposed to stay inside their rooms and it wasn't a part of the event, because it couldn't be."

"And then it snowed five inches in Florida." Ryder lifts a hand to my cheek. "The false sense of security paired with everyone being trapped here. By the time anyone *could* leave, it was already too late. I don't know what's going on, but I don't think it's pretend."

I laugh again; this time the sound is slightly delirious. "I can't believe this. *Magic*, Ryder? You honestly think magic is turning people into monsters? We can leave any time we want. We'd just have to walk to my car."

"Where?" Ryder asks.

"There's a parking lot, just further up the road. A shuttle bus brought us all over the first night."

"It's empty, and even my car is gone."

My brows furrow. "What? You've been with me the whole time. How would you know that?"

Stepping to the window, Ryder points toward where his car has been sitting dormant for days at the treeline. Just like he said—it's gone. "I noticed it missing a few days after you got sick. Things already felt off by that point, so one night after your fever broke and you were sleeping, I snuck out and followed the road. The only parking lot I came across was empty. There were no other buildings as far as I could see, and I didn't want to risk leaving you alone for too long, so I came back."

He has got to be joking.

Sighing, he faces me again. "There's no service. I've tried to call my parents and ask if they can come get us, but I haven't been able to reach anyone since I called to let them know I wasn't going to be able to make it for Christmas because something came up." His fist clenches at his side, but he takes a deep breath, shakes his head, and loosens it. "I don't know what we're dealing with, but I do know we're safe together. You understand this kind of world, and I understand how to keep us grounded. We'll make it out of this."

*Christmas magic has to come from somewhere, and with so few people left in our little village, someone has to fuel next year's…sweetness.*

Don't worry. *He'll take good care of you.*

I swallow as my heart begins to race. Dropping my gaze to the ground, I search the tile for a long moment as my memories and what Ryder is saying now all falls steadily into place. I know this kind of world? As in, a fantasy world? A story world?

Maybe I'm only thinking like this because I was reading Melanie's book before I came, but she prefaced her work in the context of our world being a catalyst for often overlooked stories. Readers like me think we explore a thousand worlds and lives because we read, but in reality we're exploring a thousand *more* than we normally would.

Life, in itself, is a million stories poured together into a trillion different scenes. The elements we cling to in fantasy come directly from the world around us, from the emotions and beauty we've already been given.

If this fantasy story is real—if it is centered around me —then…

82

It's crazy. It's absolutely bonkers to think, but it stands to reason that Ryder, my childhood best friend, has appeared for a second chance in a snowstorm whereby there was only one room left with only one bed.

He took care of me while I was sick.

We are the definition of grumpy/sunshine.

All these tropes congest around me, like they've been thrown my way, like I'm the lead character in this insanity.

"I'm the chosen one," I whisper, and then I let a laugh fall out of my mouth. I rake my fingers through my hair. "Oh, goodness, I just made myself cringe."

Ryder's gaze doesn't falter as it remains locked on me, severe and steady.

"Did you not just hear me say the most ridiculous thing in the world?" I slash my arm out. "Where's your usual cynicism?"

The door slams open, and I lurch, whipping my attention toward Jack Frost.

What the actual—

He taps inside, curled shoes and bells chiming harmlessly, hands in his pockets, smile bright on his painted cheeks. "Did someone say *cynicism*? Cynics are notoriously naughty." He glides his way to Ryder, almost like he's floating. "I know our sweet Mari isn't the cynic in here."

I don't know what compels me, but I shove myself between them, shuddering when a peppermint-cold breath whistles from Jack's lips.

"What's wrong, Mari?"

I have no idea. "We were just about to leave for the cookie contest."

"Of course." Jack Frost nods along. "Would you prefer to pair with me? We'd definitely win."

"No."

Jack's expression ices, and he cups his mouth. "*No?* Don't you know what you're risking if you end up on my bad side?" A breath of white frost leaves his lips once he's removed his hand. "We're *friends*, Mari. I don't want you dragged down by the...unexpected guest."

Icy air whips into the room, blowing the lace canopy around the bed, skating over my skin.

Oh, holy night...

A *lot* has changed since I got sick. I can't... What is going on?

Jack Frost twists on his heel, wandering to the other half of the room with all the treats I've been neglecting ever since I got better, just in case I got so sick because of an utter sugar overload. Still, even though I haven't been touching them, they've appeared fresh each day. Like magic.

Jack plucks up one of the small presents. "You still haven't opened any of these."

I go cold. I hallucinated that memory. During my fever. I dreamed it.

Jack looks at me. "Why?"

"Who are they from?" I ask.

Jack laughs, tossing the light box across the room to me.

I catch it.

"Who do you *think*?" he asks.

Santa Claus.

An evil Santa Claus.

Who may or may not have enchanted an entire village, filled it with elves, and be turning people into monsters.

Um. Wow. Okay, we're actually putting that in our list of possibilities now? Great. I've gone officially insane.

I look at the card, at the *open me*, at the reference to my favorite book. That creepy song begins to play over the speakers in my room, classical, without words, but the chiming tune that goes behind *he sees you when you're sleeping, he knows when you're awake* is unmistakably horrifying.

I look at Ryder, whose hard gaze remains wholly fixed on Jack Frost a long second before it meets my eyes.

Ryder doesn't joke around. He doesn't play pretend games. He doesn't easily freak out. He is fully grounded in reality. He looks pale.

Managing my racing heart, I pull the bow free and open the little box. The only thing inside is a slip of paper.

*My sweetheart,*

My blood turns cold.

*Wait for me.*

Dropping the box, I stride across the room, past Jack Frost, and to the table. I gather every tiny gift I can find, throwing them into a heap on one table. Twenty-three. Twenty-three boxes.

Twenty-three days until Christmas eve.

The night when Santa appears.

Heart pounding, I open one after another, after another. They all start the same way.

*My sweetheart, I'm coming for you.*

*My sweetheart, Be patient.*

*My sweetheart, I'm watching.*

*My sweetheart, I love you.*

*My sweetheart, My sweetheart, My sweetheart.*

I take back my earlier jokes. I do not, in fact, subscribe to Santa Claus romances. They are weird. I don't like them. The scraps of parchment fall from my fingers, and I jerk when a frozen hand locks around my wrist.

Jack murmurs, "That's your twenty-second one. Tomorrow's. I wouldn't risk upsetting the boss by ruining his plans."

His plans? It's…

My eyes widen as Jack's hold slips away. It's an advent calendar.

This is an advent calendar.

These gifts.

The rooms in this inn.

There are *twenty-five*. I'm in the twenty-fifth room. We've lost two people each day. I don't have time now to check whether or not it's in order, but the fact Ryder has been staying with me *here*, and he's the opposite of a ball of Christmas sunshine means something.

Evil Santa is coming for me on Christmas Eve. And then…then who knows what will happen to us on Christmas Day.

"We're friends," I say, finding too-blue eyes in a too-white face. "Right?"

Jack Frost brightens. "Of course. You, me, Pepp, Juliana, Tessa. We're all friends."

I smile. It's the only thing I can think to do.

I'm pretty sure I've lost my mind.

# CHAPTER 11

♥ There is a cookie contest, and the recipe is in the back
of the book, but it's a spoiler, so don't look at it yet.

---

I am joining the dark side. Blatantly. It's the only logical
conclusion. And it's not like it isn't what I've secretly
always wanted anyway. So long as I don't have to stab any
creeps in red suits, my terms are entirely simple.

Ryder gets out of this mess unscathed.

I'll deal with the other guests later, but first and
foremost, Ryder and Jimmy never even wanted to be here.
They don't deserve to get caught up in whatever the heck is
going on. Frankly, right now I don't know what's going on,
but if any part of this is messed up, real, or centered around
me, Ryder never signed up for it.

I throw back a swig of vodka and lean against our
counter, looking over the other "contestants" for this cookie
making contest. Before we started, I asked around to see
who was in room twenty—after determining that every
room leading up to it was empty. Room twenty appears to
be doing well so far, certainly somewhat better than the
team who literally set an oven mitt on fire. That caused a
bit of panic.

Especially when Jack Frost sighed, wandered over, and
pinched the flame out like a candle wick.

His eyes rolled toward me after, and he grinned, so I
grinned back, because I'm being recruited...by evil Santa
Claus. I seriously wonder what the end goal here is.

A curse breathes through my head, and I take another

swig as Ryder, trailed by Jimmy, returns from the shelves of ingredients lining one side of this vast kitchen space. He sets the box of candy canes I asked for down by the bowl of dry ingredients and looks at the bottle in my hand.

I lift it toward him. "Christmas spirits. Want some?"

Arching a brow, he shrugs and downs a gulp, hissing after he swallows. Covering his mouth, he coughs and croaks, "*How?*"

"How what?" I take another sip.

"How are you sipping that like apple juice?"

I turn to the bowl of wet ingredients, swap out my bottle of vodka for one of rum, and dump approximately two tablespoons into the bowl. Approximately. Part of this contest is no recipes and no measuring tools. The last thread of my sanity keeps me from dumping the entire bottle. "You get used to it after celebrating every holiday for the past five years like this."

"You…" Ryder stares at me. "What about Titus and Alana?"

"You mean your friend and your friend's girlfriend?" Deciding it's not the best idea to get drunk during *whatever* is going on, I set the alcohol aside and get to mixing my dry ingredients into my wet, folding them together until they thicken into a dough. I know how to make cookies, even without a recipe. I'm not even concerned if this contest weren't probably going to find a way to eliminate the team in room twenty.

I'm pretty sure I have what's considered plot armor.

"You were always surrounded by people," Ryder comments.

I begin scooping globs onto a greased tray. "I'm fun in small doses. You were the only person who tolerated me outside of brief interactions at school. I was sure when we started dating and spending even more time together I'd be too high energy for you, so I tried to cut back. Every other friend I ever got close enough to let down my guard in front of pulled away from me." And...I didn't want to lose Ryder.

It was my greatest fear, and he *chose* to make it come true.

Heck, maybe I'm better off with Evil Santa. At least he's putting in the effort to come to me, right?

Tessa trots over, eyes wide. "Those look amazing!"

I beam. "Don't they? They're my favorites. If I've done anything right, they'll come out soft and fluffy." Pointing my spoon at the liquor, I wink. "Probably all thanks to the *touch* of Christmas spirits."

Tessa claps, giggling.

Smiling, I move on to peeling my candy canes so I can obliterate them into festive candy topping.

Once Tessa continues toward the other counters in the row, Ryder steps closer to me, murmuring, "I never knew I was leaving you all alone."

Well. Now he does, I guess. I smile as I lock the candy canes in a plastic bag. "It's okay. It's behind us now, and I don't think I'll be alone much longer."

His brows knit. "What do you mean?"

I get the rolling pin out of the drawer of utensils. "Saint Nick's coming for me, or did we miss that part earlier?" I slam the baggy with the rolling pin, and Jimmy jumps, quacking a protest. "Sorry, Jimmy."

"You're not serious," Ryder hisses. "That was... *psychotic*."

"Yep. Just the way I like 'em. If he's ancient but looks young, everything is totally *fineee*." There is such an absence of logic in what I've just said, and I can't believe I'm only realizing it now. Fiction and reality absolutely must stay separate. I have overlooked so many red flags

89

for…what? A guy described with dark hair and a chiseled jawline? I wonder if working for Evil Santa comes with free mental health care. I might need therapy. "I hope he lets me call him Nicholas, because the mental connotations I have with Santa Claus are just…no." Seriously. What is going on? Is the guy who's sending me weird letters the Saint Nick who can be traced back to the actual person? Or is this an amalgamation of what humans have turned the concept of "Santa Claus" into? Nothing makes sense. Magic rarely makes complete sense, as the Ryder I once knew once told me numerous times, but standing inside it now is ridiculous.

It's like fourteen people got together and started describing a twilight zone, but for Christmas, and said *good luck* to whoever was then tasked to write it.

"Marigold." Ryder grips my arm, a thread of panic wound tight in his eyes.

I quit mutilating the candy canes, lift onto my toes, and kiss his prickly cheek. "It's *fine*, Ryder. I've been waiting on insanity like this my whole life. I'm prepared for just about anything mentally."

Ryder touches his cheek, whispering, "Please don't tell me your best plan is to roll with it."

I laugh and lift my rolling pin. "Ha. Roll."

"Marigold."

"My best plan is to *embrace* it. Magic world? Magic rules? Love letters from the villain? Literally one of my top ten favorite tropes. Now he just needs to show up tall, dark, and handsome instead of…well…you know. My standards are quite simple. If evil, why hot?"

The Ryder I once knew would have squirted me with water. I'm not even joking. Petulant cat is part of my character description when it comes to the fact I will die on my hill of being an attractive villain simp—and I literally might, given the circumstances.

This Ryder just stares at me before saying, "*I* love you."

I nod. "I know." And I love him, which is why—no matter what happens here—he gets out of this unscathed. Whatever comes afterward, I suppose I'll have to figure out my role to play once I figure out the genre. Christmas fantasy romance is a far cry from Christmas apocalypse.

In real life, happily ever after isn't guaranteed. I just have to remember that.

As expected, room twenty burnt their cookies into nothingness.

So Jack Frost turned them into ice.

# CHAPTER 12

♥ There is a mistletoe kiss, or something like that…

---

"*Attention remaining four participants.*" Holly's voice causes me to gasp awake—in Ryder's arms.

My heartbeat stumbles as I come to and find his face. His eyes squint open, bleary and tired. Making a soft noise, he curls closer around me, tucking his face against the top of my head. His breath skims through my hair.

Oh my goodness.

It happened.

It took twenty-three days, but it happened.

We fell asleep together on opposite sides of a massive bed and woke up in one another's arms.

If this isn't the momentary calm before the snowstorm, I don't know what is. Also, side note, I never want to leave this place.

"*Today is a very, very special day…*" Holly continues.

My stomach knots as I pull my attention off Ryder and remember everything. It's Christmas Eve. The day Santa Claus comes to town. Letting my eyes close, I tell myself to listen as I squeeze Ryder close and try to breathe in his scent.

I don't want to live in a story even if it is everything I've ever imagined and fallen in love with. Not if it's without Ryder.

"*Please be on your best behavior. There's only one last day until Christmas. Follow all the rules today. Best of luck.*"

What rules?

I don't remember there being clearly listed rules. Outside of not feeding the rescue animals chocolate.

I wait, soaking in Ryder's warmth, wondering if more information will come, but nothing does. My eyes open. How are we supposed to follow rules we don't know?

An inkling of dread wells in the pit of my chest, and I wonder if *not leaving my room* is breaking a rule. I've spent the last two days trying to come to terms with the situation, opening my tiny presents filled with creepy notes, and shuddering at the idea of being with anyone other than Ryder.

There's a reason I never *moved on* after he left. And it didn't just have to do with my heightened levels of insecurity. I never once stopped loving him. In my head and heart, there had only ever been him.

I think I understand why so many main characters pass up the tall, dark, and handsome villains now. No amount of fan service wrapped around an enigmatic villain is going to matter when you're in love with the hero.

I can't do this.

"Ryder?" I whisper.

He murmurs something unintelligible.

My heart pounds, but I rest my cheek against his chest and listen to the steady beat of his. "We need to get out of here."

He tenses, looking down at me. "What?"

I meet his eyes. "I don't want to stay here or live in a story or even be a hero. I just want to survive and be with you."

Ryder's lips part, and the drowsiness melts out of his eyes, leaving them wide. "You...want me? I'm not dreaming?"

I cup his face in my hands. "I'm sorry."

"You're sorry?" he blurts.

"I thought maybe I could do it. I thought maybe I could ask for your safety. I thought maybe I could make it work, at least save you. But now that it's *today* and I'm almost entirely certain an evil Santa Claus is coming for me, I'm sorry. I really don't want to. I don't know if we'll both be able to make it out alive, and I don't know if trying to choose you will mean I lose whatever twisted immunity I have in this, but…"

Ryder's hand closes over one of mine, holding my palm to his cheek.

"Whether you give up on me again or not someday—"

"I never gave up on you." Breath leaves him, pain twisting his brows low over his dark brown eyes. "I gave up on myself. I didn't want to be the one to break you. I wanted to let you stay the bright and beautiful thing that you are." He touches his lips to my forehead. "I wish I'd been wise enough to know how to express anything then. I'm so sorry. Whatever happens next, I want to stay with you. Even if you don't choose me, even if my future is becoming high-fructose corn syrup and food coloring, I will be right here, next to you."

My heart thuds.

Ryder just said he'd become candy for me. And it is the sweetest thing I have ever heard. Literally.

"I hope it won't come to that," I whisper. "We need to figure out a way to get away from everyone. So long as we aren't trapped in some sort of dimensional field that distorts reality, if we can sneak off and get away from the village, we'll be able to find a way back to the nearest city."

"And then? What do we do if we're followed and we bring this whole mess deeper into the world?"

"Cue Christmapocalpse 2.0. Hopefully then we'll outnumber our enemies. We'll band together all the

94

Scrooges and Grinchs of the world until we have enough negative Christmas energy to overcome the Christmas cheer. I'm almost positive people's emotions toward Christmas is where all Christmas magic comes from." I sound insane. I feel insane. I used to like Christmas before this. I used to think it was a magical time, back before real magic tainted it. I used to see it as a symbol of unity for my future family, back when I was still hoping to find one. "We'll break ornaments and burn fields of Christmas trees. I don't know."

"I'm right beside you the entire way."

Taking a deep breath, I nod, then Jimmy quacks.

The warmth in Ryder's eyes fades as he turns away from me, untangling our limbs in order to look over his should down at Jimmy's expectant eyes. Jimmy wiggles his little white tail and quacks again. Ryder pecks my forehead before slipping out of bed, and sweeping Jimmy up in his arms. "Good morning. I know. It's breakfast time. What a sad, hungry little duck you are." His attention returns to me. "Do we have a plan, gold?"

A plan would be amazing. My brow furrows as I roll myself out of bed and head to the closet. Once we get far enough away, we should have cell service again. All I really need to bring is my purse. Of course getting far enough away fast enough is going to be difficult.

This place is full of roaming dogs and cats, for some reason. Maybe they are a different kind of mythical creature? I bet they can be sent after us. And I'd never forgive myself if something bad happened to Jimmy.

No matter what, Jimmy does *not* become the best friend who gets sacrificed in the end.

We desperately need a plan. Neither of us can outrun a herd of dogs, and even if there weren't any dogs, I do not possess excessive amounts of stamina. "I don't have a plan," I whisper.

Ryder hums. "Then I suppose you'll be following my lead?"

Holding the sweater I just got out, I turn to him, "You have a plan?"

"It is my job to be the calculating one between us, isn't it?"

The tightness in my chest eases, and I grin.

❖

The plan was impossibly simple, and that should have been my first clue to the fact it would not be successful. Simple plans never work in stories.

We were going to take Jimmy "out to the pond for a swim again" right after lunch. Except we weren't going to stop at the pond. We were going to keep walking through the woods under the cover of dusk until we made it out of this mess. After all, when we took Jimmy for a swim before, we were alone—as far as I could tell. So long as I maintained my casual interest and friendly disposition throughout the morning and afternoon, none of the elves would have any reason to question me.

After all, we're friends, *right*?

We breezed through breakfast. I laughed and joked. Everything was *normal*.

Lunch went normally as well, or as normal as *normal* has been lately. Which is very much not normal. Having lunch among a bunch of candy monsters and watching the only other two humans left panic silently through plastic smiles—because *panicking* isn't very *Christmas cheer* of you—is about as normal as it has been since I got over my cold.

When they got chipped off and dragged away for *not smiling sincerely enough*, a part of me wanted to feel guilty that I wasn't sticking around in some ditch effort to save

z

96

everyone. I guess I just wasn't given the hero mindset that allows me to do a good thing without any information that it will even work out. Who knows if I'd be able to save anyone? Who knows if candy monster transformation is something that can even be undone?

Heroes are such overachievers.

All I want to do is make sure Ryder, a little duck named Jimmy, and I get out of here.

Then I'm converting to celebrating Hanukkah because, last I checked, there is no Hanukkah overlord made of magic who can ruin my holiday. There's no fanfare. No commercialized pressure. I have never heard anyone break down "the true meaning of Hanukkah" in an effort to get past all the glitz and glam suffocating the point. The true meaning doesn't get lost. It is central to the celebration.

Christmas is scary enough that we need to occasionally remind ourselves there's a *bright and gentle* meaning behind it.

A Hanukkapocalypse would never happen.

Potentially because the Jews have literally been through enough.

Pressing my lips together, I swallow and clasp my hands in front of me as I stare up at a cluster of white berries. Every life choice that has led me to this moment leaves me feeling somewhat numb. Maybe I should have fought for Ryder more when he broke up with me. Maybe I shouldn't have resigned myself to believing it was inevitable that someone else would leave me from the start.

If I'd grabbed onto him when he'd tried to walk away and told him he wasn't allowed, everything would be so different now. When that advertisement for *Christmapocalypse* came, Ryder would have stared at me, enunciated, "*Christmapocalypse,*" and I would have recalled the true meaning of common sense.

Instead, I am standing in front of the exit to Rudolph's, watched by every elf and every candy monster in the space.

"What are you waiting for?" Holly asks, grinning, over-bright.

I swallow, glancing her way before looking at…Jack Frost.

Jack Frost, otherwise known as the winter spirit who was entering while Ryder and I were leaving. The winter spirit I am now standing beneath a sprig of mistletoe with. It magically appeared while I was enjoying my tater tot casserole. And, obviously, it's a *rule* that you obey mistletoe superstitions.

Meaning Jack Frost and I have to kiss. Or else… something. Probably candy, but potentially ice. If I reject Jack Frost, I don't know if whatever role I have in this will be enough to save me from him *at least* getting mad enough to turn me into ice until Santa gets here.

Problem is: I don't think we'll get out of this if I'm ice until the boss behind everything horrible appears.

I find Ryder standing just two feet behind me holding Jimmy. His happy, snuggly duck can't dilute the agony in his eyes.

Dragging my gaze back to Jack Frost, I whisper, "Won't Santa mind?" And, yeah, that's not at all a statement I ever thought I'd be saying.

Jack grins, icy fingers locking around my chin. "I guess we'll find out, won't we? He should be here soon. The sun's setting and all."

A shuddering chill runs down my spine, and I don't know what scares me more concerning everything Jack just said. "It can just be on the cheek, right?" I offer. "Just in case."

Holly rests a hand against her heart—if she even has one. "Aw, already so loyal. How sweet."

The only person I'm loyal to is looking at me like he's presently being stabbed and whatever happens next might just twist the knife in his heart.

Jack's smile melts away, freezing over again like day-old snow, turning it sharp. "It's one little kiss, Mari. I'm offended. These are just the rules. I didn't think you had the ability to be naughty." Jack tips my face up. "There's no way the boss made a mistake, right?"

It's just one kiss. Then we get out of here.

I wring my fingers together, knit my brows, and close my eyes.

In the very next instant, several gasps fill my ears. By the time my eyes have opened again, Jack Frost is on the floor, Ryder is standing in front of me, and chairs are scratching against floorboards as a hoard of monsters rise from their seats. "Don't you dare touch her," Ryder hisses, reaching up, grabbing the mistletoe, and ripping it down. He throws the bundle, and loose berries bounce off Jack's cheeks.

The spirit of winter and ice stares a long moment before his eyes narrow.

Holly tuts, sighing.

The moment of silence lasts long enough for it to click in my brain that this is *not* good.

Jack swipes his hand over his mouth, and a plume of icy breath fans from his lips before he pushes himself up, practically floating back onto his feet. "It's the rules," he states.

"No, it's not," Ryder grits. "The *rules* are a kiss on the cheek, then you pull off a berry."

Jack rocks his head to the side, blue eyes electric. "Who makes the rules in this town?"

Ryder snatches my hand. "*Me.*"

With that, he plows out of the building and drags me

down the street. I stumble to keep up with his long strides toward the field and the woods. I can only think that we aren't going to make it, not now, not now that we've pissed off a bunch of magical creatures. And *since when* does Ryder know the rules behind *mistletoe*? Not even I knew that you were supposed to pull off a berry. I thought it sat up wherever it sits as a glorified excuse for lovers to smooch.

Tripping over my boots, I fall into Ryder, and he twists, catching me against the side that isn't holding Jimmy. His eyes lock on mine then jump over my head. He sucks in a sharp breath. "Gold, we're going to have to run."

I whip my attention behind us, at Rudolph's, and every cell in my body stills. The hoard gathers.

Ryder tips my face to meet his eyes. "Can you run?" he asks.

Not well. Not long. But I *can*.

I nod.

He grips my hand.

We plow across the yard as shouts fill the air behind us. Holly yells, "*Get them!*" and I swear a gunshot goes off. Because, oh yeah, Holly totally has a gun. That's amazing. Here I thought it was fake because aesthetics.

I am never trusting aesthetics again.

Dogs bark, and my feet slam into brittle grass before we plow into the woods. Ryder takes a sharp turn into the trees, off the path that was decorated with Christmas lights just weeks ago. Now, the sun is setting, the lights are gone, and we're being chased.

Merry Christmas?

I nearly twist my ankle on a root. "Why would you do this?" I yell, sucking in breath, battling past barren branches ready to take out an eye.

"You have to ask?" Ryder shouts.

100

"I could have survived a kiss!"

"You could have survived a kiss with a—an *ice spirit thing*? We literally *don't know that*." Ryder dives through more brush, breaking a path for me. "Ice kisses turn you into ice, gold. I'm not taking that kind of chance! Also, it's just wrong."

I can't exactly argue with him there, or on any point. Although I am astonished at the fact he knows stuff like this. Ryder *doesn't* know stuff like this. This is fantasy book stuff, my wheelhouse. He's the logical, calculating one. I'm the one who will miss three hundred moments of foreshadowing and be utterly destroyed when *gasp* he was the villain all along!

Betrayal yanks the rug out from under me every single time.

I cough, and Ryder throws a look over his shoulder at me. "Are you okay?"

No, I am running from a bunch of candy monsters through a forest at dusk. I daresay this is the least *okay* I have ever been. My legs, chest, stomach, and body are starting to burn. Wincing, I attempt to power through it.

"Gold," Ryder demands, "are you okay?"

"I'm *fine*," I exhale, and I never knew I had asthma before. Of all the things I'm learning tonight.

Ryder slows, and it's wonderful—except it isn't, because now we are pitifully jogging and we are absolutely going to get caught. Before we were just *most likely* going to get caught. Now...

Now we're stopping all together.

My thighs cry, and I want to lie down.

Ryder sets Jimmy on the ground, and my thundering heart jolts. "What are you doing? The dogs—"

Gripping my shoulders, Ryder looks me in the eye. Whatever remains of the faded sunlight leaves a purple-tinted glow across his face, in his eyes. He says, "I love you."

I can hear the trees and brush behind us rustling, the shouts, the mob, but for a precious moment it all stills, and I realize—oh. This wasn't a Christmas story, or a romantic comedy, or an apocalypse at all.

This was a tragedy.

And this is our *the end*.

"I love you, too," I whisper. "I'm sorry I asked you to stay with me. If you'd tried to leave sooner—"

His head shakes. "I *did* leave sooner, and I've regretted it every moment since. Staying with you, no matter what, is always what I should have done."

My pounding heart stammers for him, and I brace my hands against his shoulders, partly for stability, and partly to get closer. That line is almost something directly out of a romance novel, but given the fact we're about to die horribly or be turned into magical monsters, I've already more than eliminated the chance this ends happily ever after.

I guess one way of not being alone on Christmas is not *making it* to Christmas.

How's that for a plot twist, Melanie?

"I wish I had more time with you. If I could, I think I'd spend eternity with you." Tears well in my eyes, and I stand on my toes, pressing my mouth to his.

He gasps against my lips a second before returning my kiss. It's warm on this chilled night. His arms have never felt more right. His fingers slip up, into my hair, and he deepens the caress, drawing me in, keeping me close.

I remember him completely, as though he never left. I wish desperately that he'd stayed, that we'd taken a path that didn't lead to this ending, but in this moment I would give anything for a minute more.

# EPILOGUE

♥ Loneliness is one of the world's greatest antagonists.

Life is exactly like Christmas—scary and strange and exactly what you make of it. There are a hundred different ways to define its *true meaning*, but in the end it's just an excuse to find someone to love and show them every day how much.

Even if you're afraid.

Because who knows what happens next or what genre you're going to find yourself surrounded by?

Ryder breathes me in like I'm the last breath he'll ever take. His teeth nip at my bottom lip, and he relaxes into me, tugging his fingers through my hair as he frees my mouth. He sighs, his deep voice all at once calm. "You taste like sugar, gold," he whispers, kissing my cheek.

Great. I guess I've already been turned into candy. That was fast and painless. I don't feel any different either, so maybe it won't be so bad. I hope I have jelly beans on my cheeks and marshmallow fluff in my hair and pixie stick sugar on my lashes. If I must be a candy monster, I aspire to be a cute candy monster.

Slowly, I open my eyes to see if Ryder's turned into a handsome candy monster, but he looks just the same as he did before.

Well, okay...not exactly.

He's half-smirking, and that's a little unsettling. His expression is...well...uh. It's a little, exceedingly, tremendously *seductive*. Hot. Wicked, even. A touch hungry.

He's not going to eat me, right? He doesn't like candy.

Swallowing, I attempt to take a step back, but he has his arm linked firmly around my waist. He skates a finger down my cheek, and his brows dip deviously as he curls his knuckle beneath my chin. "Oh, gold…" He chuckles. "My beautiful, precious gold." His thumb swipes over my bottom lip. "Come now, love, you really haven't changed at all." He kisses away a teardrop and whispers, "You've had me scared for a moment or two—what with all this talk of *survival*." He clicks his tongue. "Please. I'm the one who prioritizes silly things like that. You've only ever known how to *live*."

Um. What is going on?

A chill runs down my spine as Jack Frost sidles into view, holding Jimmy. My entire heart combusts. He's going to hurt Jimmy! Jimmy is probably already hurt in that man's ice-cold hands! Jack snorts, petting, and Jimmy doesn't at all look troubled. "Well, this has been utterly dramatic, boss."

"Oh, shut up," Ryder mutters, letting his long lashes kiss his cheeks as he presses his lips to my forehead. "I told all of you she deserves everything. You agreed to it."

I near about choke on my saliva. "Wha—"

"Hardest I've ever worked for a Christmas bonus." Holly cackles before Tessa is tackling her in a hug.

"*Tell* me about it! But, also, it is absolutely the most fun work-cation I have *ever* gone on." She beams, eyes brilliant and sparkling.

Perfectly at ease, Ryder catches my hand and lifts his other in a flippant gesture. "Someone go on ahead and get the lights."

"'Kay, boss," Tessa chirps and darts into the darkness. In a few moments, lights explode around a clearing to streak across tables piled with food. A literal throne rests on a dais dead ahead, red plush surrounded by white flourishes.

If a Santa hat were a throne…

Ryder pulls me along, hooking Jimmy under his arm when Jack Frost offers the duck.

I peer around at the tables, the decorations, the food, *the chocolate fountain*, and my brain function ceases. I pull my hand out of Ryder's, and he casts a look over his shoulder at me, all curious wonder. As though he cannot fathom why I have yanked free of his grasp.

The man lifts a shoulder, continues up the two short steps *to his throne*, and sits, setting Jimmy in his lap and petting the little white duck's head as he reclines.

No.

Noooo.

No, no, no.

Ryder rests an elbow against the arm of his throne and braces his chin in his palm—the *picture* of hot villain arrogance.

I twitch. I scrub the tears off my cheeks. I was *not* crying three minutes ago. I did *not* believe I was turned into candy. *RYDER IS NOT FRICKEN EVIL SANTA CLAUS.*

His lips tug into a vicious smirk, and my broken brain has the *nerve* to be attracted to the menace.

"Gotcha," he murmurs, dark eyes glinting. "In more ways than one, I think."

I hiss, "*You're* Santa Claus?"

"*I'm* the boss. Santa Claus doesn't exist. And neither do elves, or ice puppets, or candy zombies." He leans a fraction forward, looking down on me. "Because, *love*, you do not like zombies."

Clutching my hands together, I stare at Ryder. And I stare. And I stare.

How? *HOW?*

Taking a deep breath, I lift my hands to my mouth, point my index fingers in front of my lips, and mute a scream. "I saw magic."

"Special effects," he notes. "Jack Frost, or should I say *Jeffery*, has been blowing smoke rings and keeping ice packs in his pockets."

Oh my word.

I let my eyes close, and it makes *too much sense* while also making none. *Everybody* was in on this *except me.* "How in the world did you afford this?"

"You remember Sir Horace?" Ryder asks.

I shake my head, letting my arms fall. "Your eccentric great uncle?"

"My eccentric rich great uncle. Who died a couple years ago. He left me a fortune and his business."

Ah. And these are his eccentric employees. Okay. Yeah. Totally not freaking out at all. Because everything makes sense now, and I bloody told him *Christmas magic* wasn't the answer.

Ryder lets his eyes close, like it's *oh so very normal* this thing that he's done. "I built you a village, wrote you a story, sent you an invite." He hums, positively delighted in that resigned manner of his. "The snow was unexpected. My car was only supposed to *break down* but be otherwise perfectly fine. I'm glad I was going slow enough Jimmy and I didn't get hurt." His eyes flash open, pinning *Jeffery* and Pepp. "I was *not* glad to see that my love had been brought out into the bitter cold."

Pepp shifts on his feet while Jeffery, no *Jack*—I'm never calling him *Jeffery*—shrugs. "We didn't have a guide for what happened that night. We were just trying to make sure everyone was okay. And, frankly, we were worried about you."

Ryder lets his eyes narrow and close again. "I suppose no one was hurt. And the fact I wrecked added a sense of realism."

I smile, my lips thinning into slivers.

A dog barks, begging for food, and I glance at the dozen or so animals littered around me, amid the Christmas party. Because it's a freaking Christmas party.

"You hate dogs," I say, because *what else am I supposed to say??* Right. I just remembered. "And cats."

Ryder, ever *so* calmly, murmurs, "You like them." The fluttery hint of a sweet smile caresses his pretty, cocky, stupid lips. "I nearly lost myself that first night here when you were holding that tiny kitten." He sighs, curses gently. "You were so precious. I had no words to describe how much I missed you and no idea how to behave after finally seeing you again."

No wonder the animals weren't trying to *eat Jimmy*. They all grew up together. Because Ryder is the one who rescued them and plopped them in this village and gave them homes.

I pout, fluttering my lashes. "You had no words and no idea how to behave? Did you forget to *write it into the script?*"

"There wasn't a script. There was a setting. And a situation. And people with characters who were instructed to meet key plot points."

Tessa lifts a hand, her mouth stuffed with cream puffs. She chirps, still dramatically *elvish*, "There were also games! We got to pick and set up and play a *bunch* of games!"

Ryder cracks an eye at Jack, mumbling, "There was also someone who took something too far."

"Our *plot point* for today was to find a way to chase you into the woods for the big reveal. I saw my opportunity and I took it." Jack lifts a hand. "I think shoving me was a bit harsh."

Remorseless, Ryder murmurs, "You deserved it."

"Rude."

My brain is flashing with warning lights. The thousand red bulbs spell out curse words in my head. I might be having a heart attack. Or a stroke. Maybe this is a cognitive seizure. I've just lost at mental Jenga, and the blocks are tumbling down. But they are made of cheese, and now a hundred mice are coming to pick away at the pile.

I have been bamboozled.

I do not know how to feel about it.

I am somewhat *immensely grateful* that the hundred people around me aren't actually paying much attention to my standing in the center of this clearing in full dubiety. I never like the idea of having a mental breakdown in public.

Getting things straight, Ryder's Uncle Horace died and left him a lot of money and a business full of weirdos who are okay with spending the month of December dressed like evil elves and candy people. He built me a village, filled it with things I like—from dogs and cats to treats and potatoes—and coordinated the most *over the top* reunion/grand gesture I have ever witnessed *in all of fiction*. He plotted himself into my most beloved role—the villain behind it all. He put me at the end of the world and tricked me into confessing how much I still want him.

My cheeks flare red, and I wish to scream. But I shall not scream. I shall speak calmly, like an adult.

Gathering my wits about me, I march to the steps and ascend to the throne.

Lazily alluring, Ryder cracks an eyelid at me, then the jerk smiles. Moving Jimmy, he grabs my hand and pulls me into his lap before plopping Jimmy down on my thighs. "What would you like for Christmas, love?"

I hug Jimmy, because I'm certain he holds the last of my sanity in his little orange feet. The darling cuddles against me, perfectly content. "You are not doing a Santa Claus shtick right now."

Ryder's smirking. "I think I might be."

Puffing a breath, I attempt to wrap my mind around this situation, and I come to the only conclusion I have been able to this entire time. "You left me."

"Worst decision of my life."

"You built me a village to apologize and wrote me into a story where I could play the lead."

He combs his fingers through my hair. "It's what you've always wanted. I could think of no better way to apologize for my idiocy after I realized my mistake."

"Your mistake being leaving me?"

"Ultimately." He traces the bumps of my spine down to my waist. "My first mistake, however, was believing I wasn't the person you wanted." He plants his palm against me. "I broke someone's arm for you in middle school. You knew *exactly* what I was. You liked the darkness. You always have. I'm the apocalypse in your Christmas. I spent years wallowing in the torment of being without you while attempting to focus on taking over Sir Horace's work. I messed up when I tried to do what I thought was the heroic thing of sparing you from myself. I never should have stopped playing your villain." He sighs. "I'm such a fool."

He is a collection of nouns I cannot rightfully say aloud while I am holding a child, that's for sure.

My heart rate might actually be stabilizing now. I guess this is preferred to being, oh, I don't know, *turned into candy or subjected to Evil Santa*. I shudder, resting against Ryder's chest in an effort to catch my breath. I cannot believe he had *flee into the woods* written out in the plan. That's just sadistic.

109

Ugh.

Crap.

I bury my face against him, breathing in his familiar scent.

I love him.

I love him so much.

I can't believe he did all of this for me. I can't believe I fell for it. I can't believe *all of this* is a pretty dang big assurance he's committed to sticking around forever. Seriously. Who builds *a village* for the girl they like and writes her a love story in tune with her favorite preferences *then lets her live it*?

He's not going anywhere. Ever. I think he might just be obsessed with me.

Ryder kisses my forehead. "I love you so much, gold. I promised you I'd prove it. I promised you I'd show you that you were worth everything to me."

I know he's not referring to the promises he made while I was delirious with a fever and he was coordinating his minions to add an extra flare of magic chaos to my foggy, sick head. I just know he isn't.

"You're impossible," I whisper.

"For you," he murmurs, "I'd make a habit of changing reality. You deserve nothing less than every impossible thing your sweet heart desires."

My heart squeezes, trembling. "I forgive you."

"For the charade or…"

"Everything." I let his heart soothe each ache inside me —including the ones I got because he *made me run*. Okay, maybe I don't *quite* forgive him for that stunt. But it's Christmas Eve, so I'll let it slide. "I can't believe you did this."

"There isn't a single thing I wouldn't do for you, gold. That's the charm about villains, isn't it?" His whisper caresses the scared, lonely pieces of my heart that crave being treasured above all else. "I'd remake the world for a taste of your lips. I adore you, gold, and my adoration has no limits."

"I don't need you to give me the world. I just need you to stay."

"Are you sure that's all you want for Christmas?"

That's all I've ever wanted.

Drawing back, I meet his eyes.

He traces the curve of my cheek, all teasing abandoned. He nods once. "I swear. I'll never attempt heroism again. I'll never do anything wrong for the right reasons again. I will be unapologetically grumpy…so long as you promise to let yourself be unapologetically bright. Loving you is not a decision I make lightly, Marigold. I have recognized the fact you have seen me and loved me as I am. Understand I have seen you down to the most whimsical part, and I am not just willing to tolerate it. I wish to embrace you, even to every extreme. You are worth that much to me and more."

A tear slides down my cheek, and he wipes it away.

From this Christmas on, I'm finally no longer going to be alone.

Gripping Ryder's coat, I press a kiss to his lips and sink into the feeling of someone loving me enough to give me everything I've ever wanted, no matter how insane. "If you *ever* try to leave again, I will hunt you down," I whisper.

His chuckle brushes against my lips. "And here I thought we didn't condone stalking."

I hum the first lines of "Santa Claus Is Coming to Town" before I steal another kiss.

And you know what?

That really is such a creepy song, but it works. Just like Christmapocalypse.

Or Ryder and I.

# JIMMY

♥ Quack.

---

*Eleven months later*

Mommy and Daddy still refuse to let me near their shiny indoor tree. They have gone so far as to erect a barrier around it in order to *protect* it. I sit in front of the fence, staring up at the lights and the strings of popcorn swirling around and around the boughs. I wonder if they understand that I am a duck.

I come from the wild. The wild is full of trees.

I fail to understand why I am not allowed near the fancy indoor tree covered in snacks.

I fail to understand a lot of what Mommy and Daddy do —particularly the face squishing. They squish their faces quite a lot. It makes me uncomfortable sometimes because I fear they forget to breathe. And if they forget to breathe long enough, I will become an orphan duck. I cannot survive alone in this world. I am too small.

"He's still staring," Mommy comments behind me where she's curled up with Daddy on the couch in our happy little cabin in the woods, right by the pond where Daddy says I was adopted. They have been curled up like that ever since they put on the moving pictures. The moving pictures are odd and scary, full of skeletons that sing, but Mommy seems to enjoy it, and as far as I can tell Daddy tolerates it because he is with Mommy.

He adores Mommy.

Daddy grumbles something nonsensical before murmuring, "He wants the popcorn."

Offended, I turn to look at my parents, who understand what I want but must have decided to hate me.

"Poor thing," Mommy says.

I am indeed a poor thing. I communicate that I am starving and sad.

Daddy sighs. "Come here, Jimmy."

Looking at the snack tree a final time, I pick myself up and toddle over to my little family. Daddy scoops me up onto his chest since Mommy is taking up the majority of his lap, and I snuggle my head against his prickly face.

"Are you falling asleep up there, Ryder?" Mommy asks, pushing herself up to peer at us.

"No," Daddy murmurs, but Daddy is lying because his eyes are completely closed.

Mommy smiles all the same in spite of Daddy's falsehood. "Long day at work?"

"I swear. Sometimes it feels like I am surrounded by elves. Impish little monsters." He yawns. "Everyone will be coming to our Christmas party on the twenty-third, just so you know. We're going to have it at the inn."

"I'll have to make a triple batch of Christmas cookies for Tessa."

"I don't know how many times I have to tell you that you can call them by their real names."

"Nope. Tessa Christmessa is forever *Charlotte's* name. She hardly looks like a Charlotte, and I have never met a *Jeffery* who acts so much like a Jack Frost before in my life." Mommy settles in and fixes her eyes back on the moving picture screen. "Did your father decide whether he wanted to have Christmas here or in the city?"

Daddy runs his fingers through Mommy's weird blond feathers. "Dad wants to come see how the village is doing now that it's actually a functional society, and Mom likes the cat community."

"Because good people like cats."

"And bad people like ducks."

I quack a protest to that because I think both Mommy and Daddy are very good people. Even though they are strange. And won't let me have the tree snacks.

Daddy chuckles. "You know we're talking about you, don't you?"

Of course I do. I'm not a birdbrain. I tell him so.

"Jimmy is smarter than both of us," Mommy, correctly, comments.

I know better than to leave snacks on a tree. I'd say my intellect is above average.

My gaze wanders back to the shiny tree. They've hung big glass ornaments all over it as a means to distract from the snacks, but I am much too smart for their misdirection. I can see the snacks clearly, and I want them. After all, I have only been fed three times today.

I am wasting away.

"Jimmy knows everything," Daddy notes.

I would not go that far.

"He does," Mommy agrees.

I protest for fear I may be required to prove these outrageous accusations. I do not know everything. I do not even know how to get past the fence imprisoning the snack tree.

"See? He agrees," Daddy coos.

I do *not* agree. I wish Mommy and Daddy understood simple words.

Mommy sits up, and I watch her wander away from the living room.

"Where are you going?" Daddy asks.

"Jimmy requires a snack."

My wee ducky heart soars. I do! I do require a snack! Thank you, Mommy!

Daddy positions himself so he can watch Mommy in the kitchen. "You spoil him too much."

I protest. I deserve to be spoiled. Daddy and Mommy both agree I am adorable. Life is hard for a little duck. Daddy says so.

Mommy returns with a bit of raw broccoli, and I wiggle up onto Daddy's shoulder as she says, "You spoil him worse."

"Do I?" Daddy locks eyes with Mommy, and I know that look. That is the look that often sends me to bed early.

Quickly, I seize my broccoli from Mommy's fingers.

"You spoil both of us." Mommy lowers her stubby beak against Daddy's egg head.

Oh dear.

The face smooshing shall commence soon. I must escape now with my quarry of broccoli.

Because I am a wise little duck, I send myself to my room, climb into bed, and dream about unguarded snack trees. Alas, it is tough to be a little duck with parents who have decided to mate for life.

Still...I wouldn't trade my little family in for all the snack trees in the world.

# How to Not Be Alone on Christmas
## Comprehensive Guide

**Step 1**: locate a convenient childhood friend driving in a snowstorm (in Florida)

**Step 2**: say NOTHING about the fact you shall become lovers

**Step 3**: encourage room scarcity at the inn

**Step 4**: make sure it's the apocalypse

**Step 5**: make sure the apocalypse is inexplicably tainted with Hallmark/small town vibes

**Step 6**: only ever eat potatoes (with a side of hot chocolate)

**Step 7**: flood your surroundings with cats and dogs

**Step 8**: add a duck named Jimmy

**Step 9**: stir

**Step 10**: fight to the death in a Christmas cookie contest (place the amalgamation of a recipe somewhere, like on the next page)

**Step 11**: be bald

**Step 12**: be grumpy

**Step 13**: be sunshine

**Step 14**: represent a body type (preferably yours)

**Step 15**: stir

**Step 16**: go on winter-themed excursions in the asbestos

**Step 17**: save Jimmy from eating popcorn

**Step 18**: insert Christmas tree

**Step 19**: insert mistletoe kiss

**Step 20**: stir

**Step 21**: go swimming in Florida

**Step 22**: survive

**Step 23**: insert plot twist

**Step 24**: question life choices

**Step 25**: Christmas.

# Christmapocalypse Cookies

**Disclaimer**: I made this up. I tried it out. Nobody died. Alcohol and dairy have been removed (because my wee family is vegan and lacks Christmas spirit). I cannot attest to the quality of a non-vegan deviation. My, how the turntables.

(I'm joking. It'll probably be fine non-vegan. It's not like I'm asking you to figure out what Chia Seeds translate to. Just like you would never ask me to effectively find a replacement for gelatin. Right? Right...?)

**Oven**: 350 (because it's always at 350, ain't it?)

**Bake Time**: 10-12 minutes feels about right...

**Makes 12** (I recommend only making three at a time in the middle of the night though.)

**Ingredients**:

| | |
|---|---|
| 1c flour | ½tsp baking powder |
| ½c brown sugar | ½tsp vanilla |
| ½tsp salt | 1 JUST egg |
| ¼tsp baking soda | ¼c softened vegan butter |

**Directions**:

1. Mix all the ingredients together with the wherewithal of an unstable elf. You want a dough. You can add a few drops of soy milk if it doesn't incorporate well.

2. Tiny ice cream scoop the batter onto a cookie tray a reliable distance apart from one another.

3. Flatten *slightly* and sprinkle a modest amount of absolutely obliterated candy cane atop (you could also mix the candy in, I think, if you want, I didn't).

4. Bake whilst staring through your oven door until the cookies appear acceptable.

5. Let cool.

6. Devour.

# Hiya Reader!

If this is the first time you've come across a Camilla Evergreen book, I'm so sorry this was your first experience with me! I promise I am normally a far more refined author who writes things that make absolute sense (lie). Generally, I don't Frankenstein books together, and I shall never do it again (lie)! Jokes aside (lie), I hope those of you who had a hand in stirring this messterpiece together enjoyed the chaos. For those of you who came along after the insanity, I might just do this again, so you'll probably want to follow me on Instagram (@authorannemilla) and keep an eye on my stories.

If this story changed your mind about joining my newsletter, first of all, wow, okay…it's a Christmas miracle (or you need therapy). And second of all, I'd love to have you on my list! I also write fantasy romance under the alias Anne Stryker, so there's a free Beauty and the Beast retelling available for subscribers (along with sales, teasers, recommendations, and another free rom-com)!

This story is a standalone, but it connects to my *How To Rom-com* series, which continues with book one *How to Fake Date Your Grumpy Boss*. I highly recommend reading the preview below.

Once again, hot deals, extra content, a fantasy freebie, a rom-com freebie, all my love, more insanity: find My Newsletter on my Instagram linktree @authorannemilla

And keep reading for that preview!

With Love & Laughs,
Camilla Evergreen

# PROLOGUE

♥ All important meetings occur in the rain, with a clap of thunder.

"To be honest," I whisper at the box of gleaming eyes beneath me, "this is not my best moment."

Rain pounds against my back, drenching my clothes, and the only thing protecting the three tiny kittens flopping around in the cardboard box under me is my awkward roof of a body. I've been hovering for five minutes in order to keep the pale orange, pure black, and little gray cats safe. My legs are starting to cramp. I don't know what to do.

Ever since I decided to leave the dorm and check out the Augustus campus at night (a *bad* decision, mind you, and one that wasn't actually even technically allowed), things have gone poorly. First, I sort of immediately got lost. This place is a town, and when you think you've left campus? Nope. You're actually still here.

I swear.

It's like a spiderweb of buildings and rolling scenery— very unlike Florida. But I did sort of expect that North Carolina wouldn't be like Florida. The Appalachians don't cut through the state for this place to be anything but hills on top of hills. As a wee Floridian bookworm who'd rather curl up in bed all day, my legs are basically broken.

I'm never doing *outside* again.

To top off the fact I got myself lost and gave myself broken legs, five minutes ago I stumbled upon this box full of kittens that couldn't be left alone. Picking them up and wandering wasn't a good idea. The last thing I needed was to break my arms along with my legs. But as I was contemplating solutions to this particular dilemma, the sky opened up and puked on me.

Books do not normally describe rain as *puke*, but forgive me for implying that the downpour hammering into my back and dirty blond hair isn't exactly like the teardrops of angels or whatever a civilized author might delineate it as. Civilized authors probably know better than to end up in such predicaments.

"Wanna know something funny?" I whisper to the cats, because if walking around with them while it wasn't pouring was a bad idea, I'm basically stuck here now.

Their big eyes are barely paying attention. Their fuzzy, floppy bodies continue to tumble about without any concern for my sacrifice on their behalf. Cats hate water. I'm sparing them from so much distress. The least they can do is look at me while I slowly lose my sanity.

"When weather is used to depict the emotions of a character, it's called 'pathetic fallacy.'" In spite of the fact I'm soaked through and about to shiver myself sick (summer nights *here* are *not* summer nights in Florida), I let the corner of my mouth hook up. "That's right. *Pathetic.* The world mocks me two-fold, and all I can do is sit here and appreciate the poetic justice."

"What are you doing?"

I leap full out of my skin when not only does a deep, masculine voice hit me in the pitch darkness all around but also when the sudden absence of rain pounding against my back sends a chill coursing completely down my spine. I squeak slightly and look up at the largest black umbrella I have ever seen attached to perhaps one of the most downright *Slenderman-esque* males I have ever witnessed.

He's tall and pale and greasy in a horrifying "don't find me alone in the woods at night" kind of way. Thick black glasses cover his eyes, and long dark hair falls around his cheeks and across his forehead. A thick brow lifts, and he's got to at least have five to seven years on me. There's nothing *teenager* about him no matter how slim he is. Heck, if he weren't in a black and azure coat boasting the giant *A* logo of this campus, I'd assume he was a teacher.

Professor.

There aren't paltry *teachers* in college.

"U-um," I croak, and if I can thank embarrassment for anything it's the fact the heat in my cheeks might be offsetting a case of pneumonia.

He notices the box under me, and both his dark brows rise. Keeping the umbrella over me, he steps to the side, angling his head to get a better look, then he makes a deep *huh* sound in his throat without so much as opening his mouth. "I take it you're not the one abandoning them?"

My mouth drops open. "I would *never.* I've wanted a cat forever, but my parents are against animals that shed. And also joy."

Once again, he makes a sound without opening his mouth—except this time it's almost like a laugh. His eyes —impressively dark in this lighting—find me past those unflattering and thick glasses of his.

When authors describe guys with *high cheekbones* and *chiseled features*, they are probably talking about this dude. Except there's a small problem with *this dude* and those *noticeably sharp* features.

He's lanky.

He's a college student.

The ramen diet leaves him on the painfully thin side.

So, obviously, all that nice bone structure is paired a bit too violently with hollow undernourishment.

If I wasn't already calling him *Slenderman Guy* in my head, now that is his official title.

"You've been talking to yourself out here for a while," he notes, casually, unlike a murderer, even if it sounds like he's been creepily watching (and listening) to me?

The distress must show on my face because he clarifies, motioning toward a building behind us. "My dorm. My room window faces this way and I was sitting in front of it at my desk when I saw you, then when I saw it start to pour."

"Oh," I murmur. I quickly rewrite *creepily watching me* to *gallantly making an effort to save me from the rain.* "Maybe you know where the dorm I'm supposed to be at is? Wellington Hall? I'm doing a college tour thing with my junior class, and I wandered outside to…get some fresh air." Technically. *Technically,* I'm out here to "get some fresh air." *Not* run away. I wasn't at all overwhelmed by my entirely female class being packed into the one big dorm room and left with little to no adult supervision. My brain wasn't at all spinning horrific possibilities into existence concerning bullying, popular girls, and me starring as the book nerd.

Slenderman Guy bristles, whispering a coarse swear. "You're a junior? In high school?"

"Yeah?"

His attention slashes over me, and the heat beneath my skin that's keeping me from frostbite ticks up a couple notches. Voice rougher than before, he murmurs, "Seventeen?"

"Yes?"

Another hissed curse, and then rain splashes against me as he fumbles with the umbrella and removing his coat. Thrusting the black and blue thing toward me, as though he's no longer comfortable looking at me, he clears his throat, opens his mouth, and closes it again. Breath pours from his nose as he finally finds words. "Your clothes are completely see-through."

Oh. Wow. Um.

I take his coat and shoot upright, stammering, "I'm so sorry." Clearly, I misjudged just how numb my legs had gone, because the second I'm up, I all but plummet into him.

Time freezes when I hit his chest.

The rain stops.

The soft *mews* of the kittens barely reach my ears. My eyes find his, and if this guy were actually Slenderman, I'd be dead.

His breath catches.

A streak of lightning illuminates a flash of his ocean blue eyes before a clap of thunder explodes in my head.

I echo a pathetic, "I'm so sorry. My legs are numb."

"Yeah?" he asks, his gaze falling before yanking back up, off me, toward the silver prongs of his umbrella. "It's fine."

I think I now get what authors mean when they describe a man's voice as *gravelly*. Up this close, he's still horrifyingly unkempt with that overgrown hair of his, and he's still way too thin to be conventionally attractive... but...he's also kind of beautiful in the same way that somber classics are.

Whoa. Okay, Rose. Let's not go there while we're using him as much-needed support against his will.

Managing to find the feeling in my legs well enough to get his jacket on, I put a tiny bit of distance between us and chew my lip. "I, um... I really appreciate the honesty. I always try to be honest. It gets me in a lot of bad and awkward situations, but I prefer knowing the truth, no matter what. Feelings can be dealt with after."

"Agreed," he says, still refusing to look at me.

I watch him for a couple seconds, surrounded in the body heat of his coat, which smells better than his too-long hair suggested it would. Something clicks inside my head, and my eyes widen. "Wait a second."

He winces.

Yeah, he *better* wince. I frown and fold my arms in the oversize sleeves; I am wearing a tent. "Were you ogling me up until you discovered I was a minor?"

Slenderman Guy clears his throat. "Not my proudest moment."

My face heats with a different kind of embarrassment, and a breath sticks in my chest as all the time-stopping magic undoes itself. It's pouring again. It's loud. The kittens are crying.

"Ogling you wasn't my intention for coming down here. I couldn't..." He blinks, and his gaze drags fingers across the canopy of his umbrella. "I couldn't see the... *details* from my window. I just saw a girl crouched in the rain."

Well, I appreciate the *honesty*. What in the world does he mean by *details* though? Against perhaps all better judgment, I turn my back on him, open the coat, and look down at myself. In another flash of lightning, I discover that while my bra is a modest white, the pink lace accents and bows are bleeding through my school uniform without a singular care in the world.

Oh. My. Word.

Curse my school for being all preppy and *wear this super thin, super sleek dress shirt* fancy. I whip the coat closed and exhale a horrified breath. Okay. Cool. A stranger saw that. A stranger was *enjoying* that before his morals kicked in. Lovely. Neat. Nice.

Help.

"Are you a bad person?" I whisper.

"Right now, probably." The sharp intake of his breath cuts through the sound of the rain. "It's not like I'm responsible for your modesty, though."

He has a point. But also basically curse him.

"Rose Briars!" Mrs. Allen shouts from over in the direction of what might be my dorm.

My eyes go huge as I look that way, and the only thing I can think is that I may very well be in *huge* trouble. "Crap," I whisper, looking at the kittens then at Slenderman Guy. "Crap."

"Rose Briars?" he asks.

"Yeah, my parents are *hilariously* oblivious to the

weight of the title they've rested upon my shoulders. I don't need to hear it from an ephebophile."

He snorts the start of a laugh and muffles it as fast as possible into a cough. The hint of a smile on his lips draws my attention a little more completely than I want to admit. "Is the pedophilia breakdown suddenly common knowledge for high school students?"

I huff. "I like words. And I like when my words are *correct*, thank you very much."

The smile that remains teasingly in place is a little distracting. It makes me forget everything.

"*Rose Briars!*" Mrs. Allen screams, the urgency ticking it up a notch.

I wince, pulled from the trance. Looking down, I clutch his coat closer around myself and shoot him a desperate look.

"Keep it," he says, like I haven't seen inside the campus store and know for a fact this thing is like eighty dollars.

"I couldn't…"

"Consider it my repentance. Also, it'll spare you from giving shows to anyone else who doesn't realize you're a baby."

My eyes roll. "I'm not a baby."

"Uh-huh."

He's infuriating. In an electric way. Ugh.

I look at the cats as Mrs. Allen screeches my name again. I'm in enough trouble as it is. "Will you take care of them?" I ask Slenderman Guy.

All the touches of humor on his face disappear. "Wha —"

"Come on. You can't just leave them here. You're an adult. It's your job to look out for the youth."

His brows shoot high up over those ugly glasses of his. "The dorms don't allow pets. It's hard to even get an ESA in here."

"Grownups are smart and figure things out."

"I'll admit I didn't expect such immediate retribution for calling you a baby."

"*Rose. Briars!*"

I jolt and dash out from under his umbrella, nearly skidding on a wet rock and falling on my face after that single step.

His hand latches onto my bicep like a vice, and, my word, ramen must be pure protein nowadays since he places me back onto my feet like I weigh nothing even though he looks like a horror story stick figure. The concern in his eyes is…sweet. Yeah. It's sweet.

I clear my throat while water pours down my face.

He releases my arm and wets his lips, glances sidelong away.

"Take care of them," I say, and before he can tell me *yes* or *no*, I'm flying across campus as fast as my broken legs will let me. I could swear I hear him say, "Take care of my coat," in response, but a boom of thunder rips all possible words away.

And, before I know it, rain-filled nights with boxes of cats and slender men holding umbrellas are little more than a memory. Like a dream. Leaving nothing behind to prove it was real except one overprice and oversize coat that has long since stopped smelling like a stranger's warmth.

# CHAPTER 1

♥ Accidents happen. It is advised that you learn to
consider them as plot points.

*Five years later*

As far as interviews go, I have to say this one *was* going well. *Was* being the key word. Of course, it all started with me screaming my head off into my pillow all alone in my dorm room so as to not disturb my three roommates. After applying to what seemed like hundreds of positions, I actually got an email back from the biggest job I'd dared inquire about, and *the* boss himself wanted to talk with me personally! It was too big an event for me to handle, so I did something I hadn't done before—I asked my roommates for help concerning exactly what one should wear to a professional interview. (Now I know better than to choose tight dresses and high heels; thanks, Sierra…)

Move steadily along to today, about an hour or two ago, and I wasn't fumbling over my words. I was answering questions intelligently. Mr. Levi Danner—young owner and founder of the multi-billion dollar corporation Leopard—genuinely seemed interested in what I had to say, what I wanted to offer, all of it. Even if the man didn't smile once.

To be fair, he still isn't smiling.

To be honest, I didn't expect his lips to be quite as soft as his body is hard. I also did not expect *either* (lips or body) to find their way beneath me.

Wide dark blue eyes stare at me as I remain in shocked paralysis on top of the gorgeous man. My brain screams at me, reminding me how I was *this close* to having my dream job if I got a call back for the next part of the interview process. Fate clearly had other plans.

Mr. Danner lies sprawled across the parking lot's black asphalt—and the fall had to have hurt even though I didn't feel it. When my high heel snapped as I was turning around to thank him for walking me to my scooter, I began a flailing tumble, and he cushioned my entire fall with his whole body.

I think I grabbed his tie on the way down because it's latched in my hand, loosened from his neck. He may have made a gagging sound a moment ago when I choked him, but I can't remember through the sound of my heart pounding in my skull. All his perfection—from his hair to his crisp, well-fitting suit—has met Hurricane Rose. And I don't even have the brain cells left to compute what exactly I've just done, what exactly I'm *still* doing.

Sense returns to me like a freight train, slamming into me hard enough to break bone. Launching my mouth off his, I jerk both my hands away from his chest and his very expensive, very *tailored* suit. I'm still straddling him, but at least my whole body isn't still squashed against him, right?

*Right?*

I can't get up.

My dress is too tight.

My...

Dropping my attention in the same moment his eyes flick down, I find that short, tight dresses don't do well in situations such as these.

Mr. Danner's throat bobs as he drags his attention away. I grip the hem of my horrid black dress and yank it down flush against his chest. "I'msosorry," I exhale in a single breath.

"Can you get off me?" he asks.

My eyes close, and I don't think I have any dignity left. "Not without help, no..."

His chest fills with air, and it's a testament to my

location on him when that action lifts me. Sitting up, my almost boss's abs flex beneath me a second before gravity drags me down into his lap. His eyelids twitch, and the irritation pouring off him in spades makes this infinite times worse.

"I'm so sorry," I whisper again, this time slow enough to enunciate each word.

"It's okay, Rose. Were you hurt?" His hand connects with my waist, and the list of reasons I hate this dress skyrockets.

I can feel every single one of his strong fingers against me. Every. Single. One. "Only my pride." And, perhaps, my chastity.

Levi Danner is *not* a kind or forgiving man. I looked into him some after I got the email confirming my interview since I don't have social media outside of Goodreads and knew next to nothing about his reputation.

At twenty-five, the internet says he dropped out of college so he could take over the world. Now, at thirty, he's more than accomplished that feat. What started as a social media platform spiraled into a hub for him to collect and coordinate hundreds of subsidiaries.

If there is something worth having, he owns a company that manufactures it. Some people speculate that it's been a game to him—a collect one of everything that exists type of thing.

His bad reputation comes from his tendency to be heartlessly blunt, allegedly arrogant, and painfully strict. He never smiles. He's never kind. People are more an inconvenience to him than anything else. His singular "shining" point is a striking lack of scandal—potentially because people are inconveniences and scandals involve dealing with them.

It's a classic case of being the smartest person in the room and being irritable because you're surrounded by idiots.

To think that just five minutes ago I was feeling smug over the fact he not only personally accepted my application to interview for the project of having me ghostwrite his autobiography but also was telling me he'd be in contact again. My idiotic heart was *soaring*.

Who, me? Could *I* possibly be accepted to ghostwrite *the* Levi Danner's autobiography? As a *sophomore in college*? Applying was a long shot, sure, but I've been looking for and applying to every single job I can find that involves words and might be flexible enough to work with my class schedule. In a deranged, sleep-deprived fever dream, I even asked the campus Taco Bell if they had any openings for putting the little letters on the little sign outside. I've seen enough grammatical errors and typos on fast food signage to last me a lifetime, and the little squirrel in me that just wanted tacos thought, "Hey, this would be a perfect job."

They could even pay me in food.

Needless to say, when I actually got the reply back from Leopard, I lost my mind. And now my clumsiness has lost me my chance.

Mr. Danner's other hand curling around my slim waist and effectively circling me in his palms draws me out of my reverie. Slowly, he maneuvers my body off him and manages to stand while helping me up. He doesn't just drop me the second I'm on my feet, though. He continues to support my weight as though I'm a delicate creature. Or a baby giraffe. Placing my hand on his shoulder, he snatches a look at my broken heel and clicks his tongue. "That's unfortunate."

"Yeah," I murmur, because I have no idea what else to say. Wait a second. There *is* something I'm supposed to say. I straighten as well as I can on my lopsided heels and look at him with wide eyes. "Are *you* hurt?"

Something almost gentle touches the deep blue in his eyes, and he stretches the shoulder I'm not relying on before running his fingers through his fringe. The perfect semi-long and pushed back styling he had going on before Hurricane Rose is looking about as mussed as his shirt now.

Honestly speaking?

The tousled look works better for him. And his clothing in disarray is not bad either.

"I'm fine, Rose."

I should probably not be thinking about the way he sounds when he says my name after I've only just finished mauling him in the parking lot outside Leopard's main base of operations—conveniently only thirty minutes away from Augustus college.

This could have been perfect.

My first real *writing* job, maybe even a *writing job* that my parents could approve of since it wouldn't have been romance or fantasy. Well, depending on this guy's life, it could have had some romance, but *autobiography* is as far from *fantasy* as it can get.

Actually, would I have even been allowed to tell them what I was working on? With the NDA, it could have been illegal for me to claim having any association with the book. And yet the pay would have meant I no longer felt this obligatory obsession with seeking out my parents' approval in the event I needed their assistance with existing. As it stands, I'm at college thanks to financial aid and scholarships. If I didn't take the gap years to save up the rest, I wouldn't be in college for creative writing—although after a year of workshops and classes that teach things I already know with a side of unnecessarily damaging criticism, I wonder if *college* was a good idea at all.

The few successes I've had can hardly compare to the soul-crushing atmosphere.

If I had gotten this job, I was going to drop out at the end of the semester and live on the cash for the rest of my life—or at least just until I could get my own freelance writing career off the ground.

"Thank you for your time, Mr. Danner," I say, unable to meet his eyes as I regain my balance well enough to hobble back toward my scooter and take a seat.

"Is it safe for you to drive like that?" he asks, and when I force myself to find the concerned gleam in his eyes, I reevaluate everything I learned about the *mean Levi Danner.*

So far, this man interviewed me personally—which seems normal considering it's his autobiography we're talking about, *but also* I'm only twenty-two and he could have marked me off as inexperienced, period. He walked me out to my vehicle—which is more considerate than anyone else I've ever interviewed with has done. He let me use his body as an impact mat—which was only slightly softer than hitting concrete because he obviously has a fitness instructor who is doing their god-given job. And now, he's worried about my driving with a broken heel.

All in all, I think I would have loved to work for him.

I offer a feeble smile and get my pink helmet off the mirror. "I don't drive in heels. That would be silly. I have sneakers in the trunk."

"Maybe next time you should stick with the sneakers throughout the duration of the time you intend to use your feet."

Ouch. I guess there's that touch of acidity people seem to focus on. Still doesn't omit the fact he saved my life here. I wince. "Yeah." Next time. "I'll keep that in mind."

His hand lifts as his eyes find their way *elsewhere.* Before I know it, his knuckle is skimming across the full cupid's bow of his upper lip, then he's scratching his cheek. "Not that your whole outfit didn't look nice. It just seems… safer."

A tingle races down to my toes, and my lips part. He just complimented me. Not only that, am I losing my mind, or did he just touch his lips? The memory of how my mouth hit his—hard, like teeth-slamming *hard*—returns, and I kick my heels off in a scramble to put them in the trunk and get my ratty old sneakers out.

Let's be clear. It was *not* a kiss. That's highly inappropriate. He's eight years older than me. *And another thing.* I'm not looking for a relationship right now. If my parents already suspect I'm getting drunk and sleeping around in college while I waste my money learning how to write things they don't approve of, the last thing I need is to be confirmed with anything that even resembles a boyfriend.

The plan they have for me is really quite simple.

First, I get a job they approve of. Like…maybe missionary work or…landscaping? (I'm uncertain what might meet their standards.) Second, I become financially stable in this economy before I'm thirty—baffling as they seem to *not* be fans of witchcraft, and only magic could accomplish this. Third, I settle down and have some kids when they're ready for grandchildren (probably through mitosis because, last I checked, sex equals bad). In case it needs to be said, my husband-to-be and I do not so much as share a kiss until we've said our vows and all our family and friends can witness the innocence of a tiny little peck.

Welp.

My lips *burn*.

Can we pretend that falling on top of someone and slamming mouths *isn't* a kiss? Because it absolutely isn't. I'm not saying I've been kissed before, but I really don't think whatever just happened counts.

I shove my socks on and follow up with my sneakers while Mr. Danners stands there, looming like a guy who is confirmed as 6'5" on Google does. You know. *Ominously.* My 5'10" has never felt so wee before. The heels helped before they committed treason.

Once I'm ready to flee with extra flee out of here, I plug the key into the ignition and start up, realizing a moment too late I've already said my *thank you for your time* line and now all I can think about is an *I'm sorry for slamming into your mouth with mine, and also potentially giving you a view of my underwear and also sitting on your chest*. Red flares into my face, and I sit perfectly motionless, like a deer trapped in headlights.

Except the headlights are deep, deep blue eyes.

Mr. Danner does the merciful thing and takes a gracious step away from my scooter. "Have a safe trip back to your dorm."

My monkey brain latches onto that. "Yes! Thank you. You t—" Monkey brain dies before finishing "too," then it starts stammering T words with vigor. Like a really old car, it coughs into action. "—ake care now!" I launch myself backward as fast as my scooter can go and nearly wipe out, to Mr. Danner's expected horror.

His dark blue eyes are wide beneath bent brows, and his arms are actually spread open as though they might have been able to catch me and my scooter if I'd fallen. Thankfully, I manage by some miracle to right the vehicle and chug out of the parking lot without any further disasters.

The moment I'm back at my dorm, I march through the common area separating four perfect bedroom and bathroom pods into each of the four corners and disappear into mine. Thankfully, Lucinda, Sierra, and Evelyn don't hear me come in, probably because Evelyn is blaring heavy metal music that conceals my arrival.

Even if we aren't really friends, girls can be curious, and since I asked for their help, they *know* where I was. But I don't want to talk about today.

I would like for today to go away.

Settling for the next best thing, I cry myself to sleep.

# CHAPTER 2

♥ A picture is worth a thousand words, and many of
them are probably curses.

What I have been doing for the past two days is something
that we are *not* going to call *moping*. Because that would be
rude and inaccurate. *Moping* denotes a level of laziness that
I simply do not present when I am depressed.

In these past two days, I have written almost thirty
pages—sixty in MLA double-spaced format. In between
catching classes and occasionally recalling that humans
need food, I have been pouring my heart out through my
fingers and making words appear for either various
assignments or various passion projects.

The Great Disaster threw me into a nervous reading
slump, so books haven't been giving me the reprieve I
need. Simply put, merely scanning words is insufficient. I
require the energy-burning therapy of typing.

My roommates assume I just completely tanked in my
interview, and they have been kind enough not to bring it
up when I shuffle out to find food.

I'm not obligated to clarify assumptions. I really don't
feel like digging back into how the best, most hopeful
moment of my life turned abruptly into the worst because I
have a chronic case of being unable to stay on my own two
feet.

It's humiliating.

I am emotionally exhausted.

So I sit. And I type. While wearing Slenderman Guy's
black and blue coat.

I don't know why the massive thing has been my go-to

comfort ever since I got it five years ago. It's probably the reason I decided on Augustus when I graduated. Not having to spend eighty bucks on a coat at another college just seemed smart. But also, I don't know what it was about him. Even given the awkward and embarrassing situation, a guy had never made me feel any kind of way before— probably because feeling *any kind of way* on account of a guy wasn't an option at home. My parents made sure that my interaction with the opposite sex was inconsequential or nonexistent.

Coming here on that school trip was the first time— ever—I had been away from the overbearing grip of my mom and dad. And someone sort of seemed to find me appealing. And maybe I kind of found him appealing, too. In a shaggy and sweet way.

I am fully prepared to believe that my silly little crush is based in naivety. I am also willing to consider that the older guy was ready to shamelessly enjoy my underwear up until hearing that it was basically illegal. I appreciate the fact he didn't just play it cool and continue his perusal while I was none the wiser. I know I come off air-headed and oblivious.

Spoiler alert: it's because I am.

I've been sheltered since the moment I was born. I was homeschooled up until high school. And then my parents put me in an all-girls private school. Movie theaters were evil. Sleepovers weren't allowed—because fathers and brothers and what if they eat *sugar*, oh my!

Reading secretly was (and is) how I lived.

So forgive me if the first guy who implied attraction then followed up with respecting my innocence brings me unnecessary amounts of comfort. Up until him, in my sheltered little box of a world, I had no idea whether or not I was even desirable as a woman. Up until him, boys and men were painted as monsters who *wouldn't* offer their coats to naive girls unless they got something out of it.

Up until him, I was used to being made fun of for my oblivious innocence, not protected.

"What the—" Evelyn curses, and the next thing I know, her door is flying open—right across the hall from mine. It takes all of two seconds for her robust form to come barreling into my room with her black phone in her hand and her eyes bulging out of her head.

I blink at her, startled and mildly concerned.

Her incredulous expression and twisted-up black lips do not bode well.

I clear my throat. "Hey…Evelyn…what's up?"

Her brows jump, the silver hoop in the left one catching the light streaming in through my window.

Like they've been summoned, Lucinda and Sierra wander in after Evelyn. Sierra—the most petite of us all—rubs her eyes like she just woke from a nap. "What's going on?"

Evelyn turns and brandishes her phone. "*This.*"

Lucinda tilts her head to get a look, and her brown curls shift against her chin before her mouth falls open. Her gaze darts between the phone and me, then she's lifting a dark hand over her full lips.

Nerves slice through my chest, and I curl deeper into my jacket.

Several painful moments slip by, then Sierra's fully awake and barking a laugh. "*Wow.*"

Wow? Wow *what*? What *wow*?

This feels familiar somehow, like I'm just waiting to be informed that the punchline to this shared joke of theirs is *me*.

I'm going to be sick.

Sierra cocks a hip and folds her arms across her chest, eyeing me deviously with baby blue eyes. "And here you had us all thinking you were innocent."

I *am* innocent. Against my will at times, but *still*. "What is it?" I whisper. "What did I do?"

Evelyn gives me a skeptical look that screams *how don't you know what you did?*

My heart pounds as she takes the necessary steps to me and shows me her phone screen.

Ice enters my bloodstream. I pale and forget how to breathe.

There, on the screen beneath a bold headline that dubs me in terms my parents would not like me to repeat, is a picture of my body on Mr. Danner's. The details are... My face is... His hands...

Oh. *Crap*.

I fly out of bed and slam into the bathroom, dry heaving in the toilet as my head spins with nervous energy. I gasp, hot throughout every inch of my skin. Tears burn and flow free as I piece things together at rapid speed.

Picture.

Mr. Danner.

Billionaire.

Me.

It's everywhere. Articles like that are *everywhere*. Mr. Levi Never-in-a-scandal Danner is suddenly beneath some strange *young* girl. Bodies pressed. Hands precariously positioned at her waist. Depending on what angles the random photographer got, my underwear might be all over the internet.

What are my parents going to think? What am I going to do?

Lucinda's hands gather up my dirty blond hair as I hover over the toilet, drool and acid dribbling down my chin. "What happened?" she murmurs, the gentle words cajoling in the chaos.

Sierra pops up onto the sink counter and crosses her legs. "Little Miss Rose Briars seduced a billionaire, that's what happened. I'm so proud."

Evelyn rolls her eyes and fixes her tattooed hands on her ample hips. "Yeah, no."

Sierra plucks her phone out and has the image pulled up from a *different* website in mere moments. "Yuh-huh. Just look at the man's eyes. I cannot blame you, girl. Levi Danner is sexy in a brooding way."

With Lucinda's help, I manage to gather myself up to my feet and wobble my way over to Sierra. I squint at her phone, letting my eyes focus through my tears as I wipe my mouth with the back of my hand.

In the image, I look wide-eyed with shock—which the kind reporters are dubbing as fake, because I'm a gold-digging prostitute putting on a show. Mr. Danner looks… entranced.

I must have missed that in the moment of complete and utter terror. I also didn't feel his hands on my hips until he was helping me off him. I squint a little harder and wonder if his hands *are* actually on my hips or if they're just kind of *hovering* there, waiting for permission. At least I haven't seen a picture with my mouth on his yet? Maybe the reporter didn't make it in time to catch that?

Evelyn gasps then grimaces and shows me her phone. "Okay. I see it now. This one *is* kind of questionable."

In this one, I'm sitting in his lap, and I'm desperately holding down my dress while I kneel around him—except that isn't entirely what it looks like in the picture. It looks like I'm trying to get my hands in all the wrong places. My head spins a bit as the image lodges itself in my brain. Dizzy, I droop into the sink, turn on the tap, and drag cold water up onto my face. "This can't be happening…"

"Maybe we should give Rose some space?" Lucinda asks, one of her hands on my back. Of my three roommates, I've known Lucinda since the start of freshman year. Evelyn and Sierra only joined us this past semester. With fall upon us, that means I've only actually known the two of them for a few months. Given the fact I'm generally poor with human interaction, I'm still working my way from *acquaintances* to *friends* with Lucinda, and I can't even tell you their last names.

Having my picture all over the internet and dubbing me as horrible things isn't going to help my chronic lack of social skills.

"I want details." Sierra grins. "What was it like? How did he *feel*?"

I only know that I still feel nauseous.

"Sierra…" Lucinda murmurs. "Come on."

"Aren't you curious at all?" Sierra accuses.

Lucinda's momentary pause leaves me feeling all alone in the world.

This is going to affect *everything*. Strangers will know. Family back home will know. My parents will know. The college will know. Can this impact my scholarships or financial aid? Surely not, right? College students do worse things daily just to quell the stress and boredom. Just… maybe they don't do those things in the public eye.

Evelyn curses, and my chest tightens as I dare peer her way. Her bold black makeup makes her expression twenty times more severe, yet I don't miss the pity in her eyes.

"What?" I whisper, not actually wanting to know.

"They've found your name."

Oh.

Great.

*Buy Now*

# By Alter Ego Anne Stryker

### Rapunzel Retelling
Crumbling Towers

### Beyond the Veil Series
Lurking in the Woods
Waiting in the Water
Wading Through Ink

### Starlight Fae Trilogy
Day of Wishes and Wonder

### Kingdom of Fairytales Peter Pan Retelling
Queen of Skies
Heiress of Stars
Throne of Feathers
Goddess of Air

# Also by Camilla Evergreen

### Historical Romance
Untempered

### Contemporary Romance
Unspoken
When Summer Flowers Bloom

### Could Have Been Sweet Rom-com Series
Could Have Been Us
Could Have Been Closer
Could Have Been Romantic
Could Have Been Real

**How to Rom-com Series**
How to Turn Your Husband into Your Book Boyfriend
How to Fake Date Your Grumpy Boss
How to Marry Your Single Dad Neighbor

Printed in Great Britain
by Amazon